BAD NEIGHBOR

M. O'KEEFE

ACKNOWLEDGMENTS

I hope you enjoy Bad Neighbor! If you want to know more about Jack and Abby, pick up BABY, COME BACK

For more information and to stay in touch sign up for my newsletter:
 http://www.molly-okeefe.com/subscribe/

Many thanks to Bold Book Design for this amazing cover, Simone Seguin for her copy-editing and formatting magic. And as ever, to Mara Leigh, Ripley Vaughan, Stephanie Doyle and Julie Kriss for being the best partners in crime.

And to you readers – thank you. Thank you so much for everything.

CHAPTER ONE

Charlotte

In the end, the futon was my downfall.

It wasn't having my sister leave for parts unknown.

Or giving her most of my money.

Or moving out of the condo I loved so much, only to move to this shithole apartment, where there was a good chance I was going to get knifed before I even got my stuff in the door.

So far, none of that had made me so much as swear. Much less cry. Or scream.

That stuff is just my life. It's the shit that happens to me. Part of being a twin to my sister.

But this futon...

This futon was a punishment from God. It was the universe laughing at me.

It was stuck in the door of my new apartment, folded up like a taco. An immoveable, three-thousand-pound taco.

And it wasn't moving.

This is just what you get for not hiring movers. Or having a boyfriend. Or anyone really, who could help move a girl with five boxes, three garbage bags, and a futon mattress to her name.

Oh, and several thousand dollars in computer and drafting equipment. All sitting safely in the corner of my apartment. I moved Izzy in first (yes, I named my system. It seemed only right, considering how much time I spend with her) and threw a sheet over her. Paranoid about this new neighborhood, I locked up between trips to my rental truck to get the rest of my stuff. Which was now all sitting behind me on the cracked cement walkway.

Except for the current bane of my existence.

The futon.

Which, I'd like to point out, I got out of the back of the truck, dragged down the path from the parking garage to this point, actually folded it up like a taco and got it halfway through the door.

But now my shaky-exhausted-unused-to-this-amount-of-work (any kind of work actually that doesn't involve a mouse, a pencil or a stylus) muscles had given up.

And to add insult to injury, my hair was getting in on the joke, by pulling out of my hair elastic and headband to pop up in white-blond corkscrews and fall into my face. It was sticking to my neck.

It was making me crazy.

Everything. Every single thing was making me crazy. After two weeks of keeping my shit together I was going to lose it. Right here.

Stop. Charlotte, you can do this.

I gave myself a little pep talk and swallowed down the primal scream of "WHAT THE FUCK HAS HAPPENED TO MY LIFE!"

"Come on," I muttered and put my back up against the

futon. I put my back against it and pushed. And got nothing. Got nowhere.

Exhausted, my legs buckled and I barely caught myself against the futon before landing flat on my butt.

I turned and pushed my face and hands against the futon, stretched my legs out behind me, and pushed with all my not-inconsiderable weight.

Suddenly, it bent sideways, throwing me nearly into the wall, and then lodged itself, half in my door and half against the metal staircase leading up to the second floor of the apartment building.

Nope. No. I wasn't going to cry. Not over this.

I just needed help.

And if the thought of actually having to talk to a human to make that help happen, seemed to me to be worse than the futon nightmare, that was just my damage.

You have to get over this, my sister used to tell me. *The world is full of people. No one lives a completely people-free life.*

The only people I used to need were my sister, the girl who made my afternoon coffee at the coffee shop on my old corner, and the fantasy of one of the guys down at the organic fruit stand near where I used to live.

But now they were all gone.

I needed new people.

And the fact that I had to find those people here, at Shady Oaks, this end-of-the-road place... well, it made me want to howl.

The small outdoor courtyard I was currently trapped in was empty. The three stories of balcony loomed over my head, the chipped paint a kind of nondescript beige. The pool in the middle—filled with a half-foot of last year's dried-up leaves and a few hundred cigarette butts—had a few busted-up lawn chairs sitting around its edge, but no one was sitting in them. The laundry area beneath the staircase directly across the courtyard from me was dark and quiet.

My new apartment was beneath the other corner stairway, a weird little shadowy enclave of privacy that the superintendent said leaked—but only when it rained.

The superintendent was more funny *sob*, than funny *ha ha*, if you asked me.

I'd never actually met the super, if you could believe that. Everything was done through email. Which at the time had seemed ideal. Now it seemed...sketchy.

Shady Oaks was a ghost town.

Normally I'd love that. But today, today I just needed a little help. Today I needed a flesh-and-blood person.

And of course there was no one.

I gave myself exactly a three count of pity. That was it. That was all I got.

One.

Two.

"What's going on?" a voice asked. A male voice. And I leaned away from the wall and looked around my futon mattress to see a ... guy.

Like a guy guy. A hot guy.

A man, really.

A very sweaty man. His frayed gray tee shirt where it stretched across his shoulders was black with sweat, and it poured down his face. He was my height, maybe a few inches taller. Which in the world of dudes made him kind of short. But he was thick and square, giving the impression that he was taller than he was. And bigger.

Did I say big?

While I watched, he lifted the bottom edge of his shirt and wiped his forehead, revealing that even his six-pack abs were sweating.

"You gonna move this thing?" he asked, scowling at me while I stared at his abs.

I blew a curl out of my face and tried for my best cheerful tone. I even smiled.

"Trying to. But I think the futon likes it here."

"I can't get into my apartment," he said. Ignoring my joke, he pointed at the door next to mine, the door he couldn't get to past the futon barricade.

"Oh," I said, inanely, trying not to stare at his sweat or his body. "We're neighbors."

"Yeah. What are you doing with the futon?"

"Well, you're welcome to try and reason with it, but I've found it very disagreeable—"

"You moving it in or out?" he asked. My charm completely not charming to him.

"In—"

With one hand—*one hand*—he shoved the futon into my apartment. After it squeezed through the door it flopped open in the middle of my white-tiled kitchen.

I leaned into my doorway.

"Wow," was all I could say.

"You want it there?" he asked.

"In my kitchen?" I laughed. "While I can appreciate the commute for coffee—"

Sweaty grumpy guy had dark brown eyes—Pantone color 0937 TCX, if I was being exact—set wide in a flushed face, and I only got a glimpse of them before he was inside my apartment.

Without asking, he just stomped right in.

"Wait...what?"

"Bedroom?" he asked.

I blinked at him, thinking of my livelihood under the sheet in the corner, and if he tried to rob me I wouldn't be able to stop him.

I wouldn't be able to stop him from doing...anything.

And I'd had that fantasy about the guys at the fruit stand locking me inside the store with all of them. But this was not that.

This was Shady Oaks, and a burly stranger just walking into my apartment like he had that kind of right.

"Do you want this in your bedroom?" He said it slowly, like I was an idiot.

"You don't have to do this."

"You can't do it." His eyes skated across my body, taking in my paint-splattered overalls and the hot pink tank top I wore underneath it.

He couldn't see that my tank top had Big Bird on it. But he looked at me like he knew.

He looked at me like I had a sign that said *185-pound weakling* on it.

"I'm putting it in your bedroom."

And he took the futon by the corner, like the hand of a misbehaving child, and dragged it through my shabby kitchen, past the living room with its bank of barred windows, and then into my bedroom. I followed but stopped in the living room by the sheet-covered Izzy, as if to keep her calm, or to stand in his way in case he tried to touch her.

I could just see the shadow of him in my bedroom as he all but tossed my futon onto the floor.

Funny how he was doing a nice thing, but still I managed to feel both threatened and insulted.

Deep breath, Charlotte, I told myself. *Deep breath*.

He was out a second later, standing in the doorway of my bedroom, thick and square. His damp shirt clung to every muscle. And he had...he had a lot of muscles. Thick round knobs of them. Lean, hard planes of them. He was made of muscles.

He'd been running, or working out or something. He wore

running shoes and athletic shorts that were frayed in the same well-used way his shirt was. White earbuds had been tucked into the waistband of his shorts, and dangled down by his...well. Shorts.

His black hair was buzzcut short, down practically to his scalp. And his face, now that the flush was gone and the sweat had slowed down, looked like it had recently taken a beating. His eye was dark and his lip had a cut. His nose looked like it had been broken a few times.

He carried himself like a guy who lived in his whole body. Like every molecule was under his control. I lived in exactly 12% of my body. I wasn't even sure what my hair was doing.

"You done?" he asked.

"Moving?"

"Staring."

All the blood in my body roared to my face. My stomach curled into a ball like a wounded hedgehog trying to protect itself from further harm.

"Thank you," I said, staring intently at the edge of a tile in my kitchen. It was chipped, the white enamel long gone. "That was nice of you to help."

"No big deal." He stepped into the living room and I went back against the wall, giving him a wide, wide berth. Wanting to keep as much distance between us as I could.

He stopped. "What are you doing?"

"Nothing."

"You think I'm going to hurt you?"

"I'm not sure what you're going to do."

He made a grunting noise and stood there like he was waiting for me to look at him, but I did not. I burned under his gaze and fussed with my sheet, wishing Izzy was set up so I could just work, instead of... this.

Instead of being human with humans.

And then he was gone. Leaving behind the smell of man.

And sweat. And it was not a bad smell. It was just different, and it did not belong in my space.

I folded forward at the waist, sucking in a breath.

Jeez. Wow.

That dude was potent.

And I was pretty much an idiot.

I walked into the bedroom and used all of my strength to slide the futon out of the middle of the room and against the wall. There was another thump in the living room, and I realized with my heart in my throat that I'd left my door open. I ran out only to find my sheet still over Izzy, but the rest of my stuff had been brought in.

Two big boxes and the garbage bags.

He'd moved the rest of my stuff in and then he left.

That was...nice.

Unexpected and nice.

Neighborly, even.

I thought about knocking on his door to say thank you. It was what I should do. It was the right thing to do. Neighborly. It was what my sister would have done.

My sister would have gone over and thanked him and then probably screwed him.

But I was not that person. I was the opposite of that person.

Silently, like he could hear me—and maybe he could, I had no idea how thick these walls were—I stepped to my door and then shut it.

And then locked it.

And chained it.

Taking a deep breath, I turned and looked at my new home, with its chipped tile and the barred windows. The bare lightbulbs hanging from the ceiling. Outside, there was a siren and a dog barking.

Next door, my neighbor turned on his stereo, answering the question regarding how thick my walls were. Paper thin.

For a moment the grief and the panic and fear were overwhelming. Tears burned behind my eyes and I couldn't take a deep breath. But I pushed the panic back. Smothered it. Just set it aside like a bag I didn't want to carry anymore. I had so many of those kinds of bags, all along the edges of my life.

I closed my eyes and searched for calm.

Deep breath, Charlotte. This is not so bad. This is not forever. This is not permanent. This place is not your world.

I opened my eyes and took in my new home again, with my rose-colored glasses fully in place.

It wasn't so bad here. The hardwood floors in the living room and bedroom were nice. A coat of paint. Some curtains to hide the bars. My coffee pot. Izzy up and humming in the corner.

It would feel like home. It would.

I could ignore the neighbor. I was good at ignoring actual humans.

As bad as this place was, and it was bad, I had to remind myself that it was actually perfect.

Because no one—even if they were looking—would find me here.

And my sister was okay. She was safe.

Which was all that mattered.

CHAPTER TWO

Charlotte

The next morning I woke up to the sounds of Mrs. Athens upstairs, yelling at her girls to get ready for school.

"Put your shoes on!" she yelled, just like she yelled every morning. "How many times do I have to tell you?"

Several more times. I could vouch for that. You'd think her kids had an allergy to shoes.

I opened one eyelid and glanced at the clock. 8:10. Like clockwork. Every morning.

But then I rolled over onto my back, and my ceiling was one giant water stain, the color of weak tea, and through it all ran a spiderweb of cracks.

Oh. That's right.

I was not in my beautiful condo, with its balcony and the red geraniums. The kitchen with all the pretty appliances I never used.

I was in Shady Oaks apartment 1B, and I'd spent most of

the night worrying about the strength of the bars on the windows.

Well, no matter where I was, work had to be done. And it was oddly comforting that in my new apartment I lived beneath a mom getting her kids ready for school, just like my old condo. How bad could Shady Oaks be if there were moms here yelling at their kids to put on their shoes?

I got out of bed and put on the coffee and decided instead of setting up Izzy and getting lost in work, I would use the rest of the time on my rental truck and spend some time making my hovel a little more like a home. So, I checked my meager bank balance, remembered fondly when I used to be rich, finished my coffee and took a deep breath at the door.

I didn't like thinking about what was out there. Not just the empty pool and the vacant apartments, but *him*.

His broken nose, and sweaty abs, and deep brown eyes that ruffled through my clothes while I was wearing them, and I did not want to leave this place in fear of running into my neighbor.

It was ludicrous, the mark he made on me. When I undoubtedly made no mark at all.

Which frankly was the reality of my life.

The world and its humans dented me and chipped my paint, and tore off a layer of my skin and made me feel...damaged.

And I worked so hard to just make an impression. And usually failed.

Back in my old neighborhood, I'd go to the same place every afternoon to get an iced coffee from the same girl. Every day. And every day I got a blank stare and a "can I get your name?"

Every. Day.

And I was pretty fragile right now, not sure how much more skin I could lose before I'd start to bleed, and I thought of my neighbor and his body and the way he said "you can't do it," and I prayed: *Please, please please don't be out there. Please.*

I unlocked my locks, undid my chain, and opened my door a crack only to find the empty, Bay-Area-in-end-of-September, sun-splashed courtyard.

No next-door neighbor.

No anyone.

Yay, for small victories.

From my corner of the apartment complex there was a cracked cement path to an underground parking garage, where I'd put the rental truck I'd rented for 24 hours.

When I gave my sister the majority of my money, including what came from selling my condo in the span of a week, I kept just enough aside to live until my next advance check.

Abigail insisted that I do that. I would have given her everything, and she knew that.

So she just took most.

Which frankly was the mathematics of our relationship—I would give her everything, she only took most.

But at the hardware store—as I piled cans of paint and brand new shower curtains and bath mats that looked like frogs into my cart—I was glad, once again, for Abigail.

Who only took most.

Back in my apartment, I put Izzy in the middle of the room and rolled some paint onto the walls. A pale yellow color for the living room that made the most of the sunlight and—I thought—the dark bars on the windows. My bedroom was transformed by a pale lilac color, which I spread over the ceiling too, getting rid of the tea-colored water stain. The little bit of the kitchen not covered in tile, I painted bright red. Vivid red.

High on paint fumes, I stood back and admired my work.

Not bad, not bad at all.

I set up my easels, and clipped the color scheme and character sketches for the book to them. I put some shades over my bare light bulbs. Some adorable bumblebee curtains went up over my windows.

There were a few problems. My shower head didn't work. The exhaust fan over my stove didn't work. The doorknob on my bedroom door kept falling out. Minor, I told myself as the little problems began to stack up. All minor.

By my second night in the apartment—the dump started to feel like *my* dump. A place I could live and work, even if only for a few weeks. Months at most.

So, relief making a giddy mess of me, I set up Izzy. To get reconnected to my life. My world.

My desk went up first, which was basically an Ikea dining room table with screw-in legs and a chrome desktop. I set up my two monitors, my scanner, my tablet. My hard drive. Drawers and drawers of pens and paper. Watercolors.

Happier every minute, one by one I plugged everything into my power strip. And then plugged my power strip into the wall.

And blew out all the power.

My entire apartment went black. A little girl in the apartment above me screamed and I figured it wasn't just my apartment.

Shit.

Me and Izzy blew a fuse. Had to be.

I found my phone and called the superintendent. Nick—who when I signed the lease said someone on the staff would be available 24/7. So, of course the call went right to voice mail.

"Hey Nick," I said, leaving a message. "We've got a power outage problem. Me and I think the apartment above me."

I hung up and opened my door only to find the courtyard

was full of people. Everyone on my side of the square apartment building muttered about their power having gone off.

I put a blackout on half the place.

Great. Just great.

Well, my dad raised me right, and I knew how to replace a fuse or flip a breaker. I just needed to find the box. And nestled into the back end of the staircase leading up to the second floor was a door with a sign on it that said: *Basement. Keep Out.*

Basements were where the fuse boxes were.

I grabbed my flashlight and keys, locked up behind me and tried the doorknob to the basement, surprised to find it turned and the heavy metal door swung open.

The stairs leading into the basement were dark and frankly, the stuff horror movies are made of. There were cobwebs with actual spiders in them. I could hear something wet dripping down there.

A couple of human screams and the scene would be perfect.

The urge to go back to my apartment was a taste in the back of my throat. But my father did raise me right, and a bunch of people were out of power because of me and I couldn't chicken out.

I put my foot down on the first step, and it creaked and echoed.

So did the second and the third.

My breath was rattling in my throat.

Behind me there was a cheer, and I glanced over my shoulder to see lights coming on in the windows again. Oh thank God, Mission Fuse Box could be aborted. But before I could turn and spring up the stairs I was blinded by a flashlight below me pointed right in my face.

"Hey!" I muttered, turning my face aside.

"What the fuck are you doing?"

Great. Grumpy, sweaty neighbor.

"Can't you read?" he asked. "Sign on the door says keep out."

My vision was still blasted from the flashlight, but I could hear him coming up the steps and I turned and ran out of there, tripping on the second step, catching myself on the first and I imagined in a split second the sight of my ass bent over and illuminated like a full moon.

By him.

Like I had wings on my feet, I got out of there and stepped sideways to my door. He came out behind me, wearing another sweaty tee shirt and another pair of athletic shorts. He locked the door to the basement and turned to face me.

"Don't go down there," he said.

"Why do you have a key?" I asked, flustered and angry.

"Because I do."

"Can I have a key?"

"No."

"Does Nick?"

"Nick," he said with a laugh, "doesn't do shit like this."

"Well, that would have been lovely information to have before signing the lease. I have a bunch of things I need fixed in my apartment," I said rather inanely.

"Nick's not a super."

I was realizing this now.

"Is there stuff in the basement?"

I turned back toward the locked basement door, but my neighbor got in my way.

"What do you need?"

I blinked at him.

"What do you need fixed in your apartment?"

"Nothing, really. I mean not anything big or whatever—"

"Do you have things you need done or not?" he snapped like I was wasting his time.

"My shower head, my bedroom door, and the fan over my stove. None of them work."

"I'll take a look."

"What?" I shrieked it. I did. He looked up at me wide-eyed.

"You need shit fixed? I can probably fix it."

"That's not...your job."

"How do you know? Maybe it is. Let me get my tools."

I had a vision all of a sudden of him shirtless, with a tool-belt around his waist, standing in my bedroom, and I was speechless just long enough for him to walk to his apartment without me stopping him.

I unlocked my door and then he was behind me, stepping into my apartment, a hot breath all along my back.

"You work fast."

He was looking at all my stuff, my red kitchen and bumblebee curtains. My easels with my character sketches and color palates.

Izzy.

"You should open some windows or something. These paint fumes are gonna make you sick."

"I'm okay," I said. Though I felt a little high.

"I'm leaving the door open," he said.

That vein of conversation petered out pretty hard.

"I didn't thank you yesterday for helping me move my stuff in."

"Yeah you did."

"Not the second trip. You didn't have to do that."

"Nope. I didn't. What do you want me to work on first?"

This guy made no sense. Rude but helpful. Offended, somehow, by me while at the same time being so offensive.

"1B?" he called me by my apartment number. "What first?"

"Stove fan." I pointed at my stove just in case he missed it. "Right over there." Further instructions, like he was going to get lost in my miniscule apartment that was probably the exact same as his miniscule apartment.

His tool box made a heavy thump on my kitchen counter and he leaned over my stove. I gave myself a good eye-rolling.

"I don't even know your name," I said.

"I don't know yours either."

"Do you want to change that?" I asked with a laugh.

"I don't know. 1B has a ring to it."

"Is that... are you joking with me?"

"You started it."

He was! He was joking. Maybe grumpy neighbor wasn't so grumpy after all. Maybe he was just socially awkward—which I totally understood. I could be socially awkward in an empty room.

"Charlotte," I said. "That's my name." I didn't tell him my last name. Maybe I shouldn't have told him my first name. I had no idea how this living in hiding thing worked. Was I supposed to have an alias? Set up some other kind of life? That might be fun.

Who would I be if I wasn't me?

He looked over his shoulder at me, as if he was gauging whether the name fit. It did. I was a Charlotte through and through. He nodded as if agreeing, and then went back to taking my fan apart.

"I'm Jesse," he said. "Jesse Herrera."

Jesse fit him too, in a way.

"So, you work for the apartment building?" I asked. "Like a handyman?"

"No."

"You're just being neighborly?"

He was silent, as if answering a kind of larger existential question. And then he was silent for so long it was obvious he wasn't going to answer.

All right. Jesse didn't want to talk. No big deal.

Except the problem was, with other humans I wasn't very good at silence. By myself I lived in total quiet, but if there was silence between me and another person I felt painfully compelled to fill it.

"How long have you lived here?" I asked, unable to help myself.

"A few years."

"Always in that apartment?"

I felt his answering grunt indicated a yes.

"What's the deal with the basement?"

He paused, his hands still on the fan he was taking out of my range hood. "There's no deal. You just need to stay out of it."

"Bodies?" I joked. "Is that where the bodies are?"

He turned to face me, his entire body coiled. Or poised. His eyes met mine and I felt my heartbeat behind my ribs. His attention was heavy. Calming, kind of. Like one of those jackets you put on dogs who are terrified of fireworks on the fourth of July. I took a deep breath and felt some of the nerves alive in my stomach settle down.

Weird. Other people did not calm me down. As a rule, they stirred me up. And good-looking guys? They made all my dorky come out.

"Charlotte." His voice saying my name was one of the most intimate things I'd ever experienced. It was like I was standing there with my clothes off.

"Wh...what?"

"You can't go in the basement. Pretend like it's not even there."

"Why?"

"Because there's stuff down there that you don't want to know about."

I didn't want to know about any of this, frankly. I wanted my Nob Hill condo back with the coffee girl who didn't know my name.

"Okay," I said. He made a sound that might have been a laugh. "What?" I asked. "You said don't go down there and I agreed."

"I expected you to argue."

"Have I given you the impression that I argue?"

"You're arguing with me right now."

And so I was.

"Well, I want nothing to do with the scary basement. It's all yours."

He turned back to his fan and I turned back to Izzy and found my other power cord and my extension cord and started splitting my equipment up, trying to pretend like he wasn't even in the room with me.

It lasted five minutes.

"Do you do this kind of thing for everyone?" I asked.

"No. You're special." He was being sarcastic and that shut my mouth. I plugged in one power cord and then ran my extension cord into my bedroom and plugged it in there.

The lights stayed on.

Small victories.

"That's quite a setup," he said when I came back to my desk.

"Are you talking about my computer?"

"It's the only thing in the room."

It was true. I didn't have a table. Or a chair. Or a couch. I had Izzy. And the easels.

"Setup like that makes me wonder what the fuck you're doing in a place like this?" he asked, the muscles in his forearm twitching and turning as he unscrewed things on the fan.

"What do you mean?"

"That's gotta be worth some money. Most people would sell it and do everything they could to avoid Shady Oaks."

"It's not that bad."

He laughed. I smiled. Both of us in on the joke. Shady Oaks was pretty fucking bad.

"I won't be here long," I said.

"Funny. I said the same thing when I moved in. Most people do."

Well, that was sobering. I wondered how he ended up here, and all the things he'd done to try and stop himself from landing at Shady Oaks. But I wasn't brave enough to ask. Because I wasn't brave enough to hear the answer.

"So?" he asked. "How did you end up here?"

My sister fell in love with a sociopath and I had to give her all my money so she could get away from him. You know. The usual.

"Boyfriend kicked me out," I said instead. Because I was being the opposite of me.

"For real?"

"It's so hard to believe I have a boyfriend?"

"It's hard to believe he'd kick you out."

That...whoa. That was kind of a compliment? Like a flirty compliment thing? All of a sudden I didn't know what to do with my hands, so I put them to work starting my computer. Setting everything up just the way I liked.

"What do you do with all that stuff?" he asked, waving his screwdriver at Izzy.

Hmmmm...truth or lie. Truth or lie.

"Live chat porn."

I mean, if you're gonna lie, you gotta really go for it, right?

"What?"

"You know, guys call in—"

"Bullshit. Total bullshit."

"How do you know?" Perhaps it was the way I was blushing.

"Live chat porn doesn't have easels."

I sighed. "Good point."

"And you look like a kindergarten teacher."

Believe it or not, that was not the first time I'd heard that comparison.

"Kindergarten teachers can't do porn? It's a kink thing."

"Oh, I get the kink," he said, glancing at me sideways before returning to his work. "I just don't think *you* are doing live chats."

See? That didn't sound or feel like a compliment. This guy couldn't pick a lane.

"I'm an illustrator and designer," I confessed. Trying to be someone else had lasted about five seconds.

"What do you design?" he asked.

"Well, right now I'm working on a book."

"You're designing a book?"

"Maybe you've heard of them." I meant it as a joke, but as the words came out of my mouth I realized how mean they sounded. How I was judging him. Or how I had judged him and didn't even realize it.

Luckily he didn't get offended. "One or two," he said, real dry.

"It's a kind of a *Where's Waldo* thing."

"The kids' book?"

"Yeah, but with Jane Austen. So it's not really for kids. Unless they're like really smart kids. Or maybe weird. I don't know. I would have liked it as a kid, but I was a weird kid." Rambling. This was me rambling. He was silently putting my fan back together, so I just kept talking. Filling in the silence with noise. "But I'm creating all these page layouts that are time and period appropriate and hiding Jane Austen in them.

Right now I'm working on Hyde Park and stumped trying to pick which part of the park to use. The Serpentine Lakes? The Rose Garden? It's an embarrassment of riches, actually."

There was no way he gave a shit about Jane Austen or Hyde Park. But I couldn't stop talking.

"I just finished the Almack's Assembly rooms. That was kind of fun. I have all these couples making out behind ferns. I figured that had to be fairly accurate. I mean, that's what they do in romance novels."

SHUT YOUR MOUTH NOW! I yelled at myself. But nope, I just kept on talking.

"And I've done a garden tea party and I'm going to do Buckingham Palace and Newgate prison..."

Suddenly, he put down a screwdriver and hit the button for my exhaust and the fan whirred to life.

"You fixed it!" I squealed, in a weird relief to not be talking about Jane Austen anymore.

"You don't need to sound so surprised." He wasn't smiling, his mouth was a firm line. But he gave the *impression* of smiling, a certain lightness in his eyes maybe.

For a second we were silent, each of us just looking at each other, and I was so busy taking him in, soaking in that hint of a smile he was giving me, that I forgot to feel self-conscious. I forgot to suck in my belly or run my hand over my hair, I just stood there and let him look at me.

While I stared at him.

He wasn't just hot. He was handsome. His face chiseled, his jaw hard. His lips, even in that line, were thick and full. The kind of lips I could pinch in my fingers.

Bite with my teeth.

"Bedroom?" he asked, jerking his thumb toward the shadowed doorway beside my kitchen.

I opened my mouth to say *what* but nothing came out.

Was this the fruit stand fantasy coming true? Was this...

possible? He said *bedroom* and I just led him in there and we went at it? Was that how these things worked?

Maybe in my sister's life. But not mine.

But it could be. Right now. I could do it.

Shady Oaks was pretty much a turning point in my life. If I was ever going to NOT be me, this was my moment.

"You said something about the doorknob?" he asked, and I nearly sagged against my desk. Right. Of course. He wasn't talking about having sex with me in my bedroom, he was talking about fixing my doorknob.

"The doorknob falls out," I said, my voice weird.

He vanished into my bedroom and I imagined him in there with my rumpled bed. The dent in my pillow from my head. I imagined walking in that shadowed room and taking off my shirt. Pressing my breasts against his wide, muscled back. I imagined putting my hands around his waist and he would grab my wrist, dragging my hand down into his pants. He would swear under his breath.

Damn.

No, hotter.

Fuck.

Yes, he would say *fuck*.

He would turn around and push me down onto my knees.

And I would go. Oh my god, I would go to my knees so fast I'd get bruises.

This was worse than the fruit stand thing. So much worse.

Or better? Whatever. It was sharper than that old fuzzy fantasy. This was bright and hot and so clear in my brain it ricocheted through my body.

"What else?" he asked, coming into the room, and I jumped practically out of my seat.

I was being an asshole, making jokes about him not reading and then fantasizing about having anonymous sex with him. These were new lows for me.

"Nothing." I wanted him out of there. Wanted him out of my space. Wanted to stop imagining what was underneath those athletic shorts.

"The shower head?" he asked, ignoring my nothing, and stepped into my bathroom. I closed my eyes and put my head in my hand.

While I'd been behaving like a total idiot, my computer had been booting up, and little alerts started binging all over the place.

Updates and emails.

A new Facebook message.

My heart stopped and my blood went cold. Jesse in my bathroom all of a sudden ceased to exist.

Only my sister Facebook messaged me, and she was far away. Supposed to be off the grid. Hiding. I was not supposed to know where she was, not for a few months anyway. Those were her rules, not mine.

No, I thought. No, Abby, don't do this.

I clicked through my screens, opening up Facebook, and saw that I had a message request from someone using the name Cheetara.

Goddamnit.

It could only be my sister and a shitty code.

We'd been idiots for reruns of that old *Thundercats* cartoon.

"Hey." Jesse startled me from thoughts of my sister and I stood up, clicking shut the message request. I hadn't accepted it. But I hadn't rejected it either.

Because my sister was a selfish princess.

But I was a fool.

"Jesse!" I said too fast. Too bright. My hands were shaking. Everything was shaking and I would have given everything, nearly everything I had left in my life, for him to walk across that room and hug me.

Just hug me.

Because I was scared and I was really...really...alone.

"You okay?" he asked. "You look...scared?"

"I'm fine," I told him, attempting to laugh, but he clearly didn't buy it.

"What happened?" he asked, looking around like there was some bad guy in the corner of my room he would protect me from.

"Nothing," I whispered, feeling myself splinter at the edges. The pressure finally too much for my rose-colored glasses. "I mean...my life happened. My life just keeps on happening."

It was too much. I was saying too much. I pressed my lips together, keeping everything inside.

"Life does that," he said, and I laughed and then swallowed it when it turned into a sob. I turned away, so embarrassed, so completely embarrassed to be breaking down in front of him.

"Your shower head is fixed," he said, like he knew if he pushed me I'd crack. And there was no coming back from cracking at Shady Oaks. If I fell apart here, I didn't know how to put myself back together. I had no resources. No secret stockpiles of strength and good humor and foolish optimism.

I took a deep breath and then another, and finally when I had myself in hand I turned to face him, the awkwardest smile ever glued to my face.

"How much do I owe you?" His face was literally unreadable and I had no idea what he was thinking.

Probably something along the lines of: *oh, get me the fuck away from this crazy lady*.

"Don't worry about it."

"Well, that doesn't seem fair. I owe you something." My skin got hot as I thought about getting on my knees in front of him. I would do that now if he asked. I wanted him to ask.

I would do anything he asked, that's how much I ached for some kind of connection. Some kind of real. And his eyes widened, his face tightened, because he knew it.

My loneliness was in the air. My desire. My grief.

Please, I thought. *Please touch me.*

"Stay out of the basement," he said, and I jerked at his words.

"That's it?"

"It would mean a lot." He opened my door, and outside I saw that it had started raining. Droplets splattered against his shirt as he stepped outside. "And...you could show me that picture you're working on. The woman hiding in the park."

Jane Austen in Hyde Park.

I very nearly gasped.

And then the door was shut and he was gone. And my apartment seemed very empty. And I felt very alone. My face burned, my body ached.

I collapsed into my chair and clicked open Facebook again so I could stare at my sister's message.

How like her. How fucking like her. To not play by the rules, or to think that the rules didn't apply to her. Sure, I could rip my life apart and give her just about everything I had, with the express understanding that she...LIE LOW!

And within a week she's on Facebook.

This wasn't lying low.

This was going to get us both found.

And both of us killed.

CHAPTER THREE

Jesse

Idiot. What a fucking idiot.

I put my tools back in the cupboard underneath the sink in my own kitchen and called myself a few more names.

This whole fucking thing worked because I talked to no one. Looked at no one. I let people watch me out of the corner of their eyes and whisper about me behind their hands to each other.

I pretended I didn't know the rumors. Didn't care about the rumors. I fucking cultivated the rumors.

That I was trouble. Dangerous.

In a place full of people hiding from something, living on the dark edges of the world so the shit they did wouldn't get noticed, I stood out.

I stood out as someone nobody wanted to mess with.

And that suited me and my boss just fucking fine.

But Charlotte...

She was like a piece of dandelion fluff. Fuzzy and scattered.

Light as goddamn air.

Soft. I didn't have to touch her to know she would be soft. Her skin. Her hair. All of her.

She had fucking bumblebees on her curtains.

And something had happened while I'd been in the bathroom. Something that made her want to cry. Something that hurt her.

And I should not give a shit. Not giving a shit was the thing I excelled at.

But I came out of that bathroom and saw her big blue eyes filled with tears and... I gave a shit.

This world, this place—it was going to chew her up. And for a moment there... a moment, I'd wanted to stand in between her and everything Shady Oaks would do to her. I wanted to stand between her and whatever had hurt her.

And she knew enough to be nervous about me, but she couldn't quite hide her fascination. Whatever she'd been thinking about me while I'd been in her bedroom—it had been hot. She'd been blushing so hard and so red, all across her cheeks and down her neck. I wanted to unbutton that pretty pink shirt she wore and see how far down that blush went.

Jesus God. Her skin would be soft.

And I hadn't had anything soft in my life in a real long time.

And that, that right there was a problem.

Because I'd stopped wanting soft. Stopped even thinking about it. Forgot it existed.

It was a problem because I didn't know who the fuck that Jane Austen woman was. And I didn't give a shit about a garden, but I wanted to see that picture.

And I really, really wanted to touch Charlotte's skin.

Soft, and all its temptations, moved in *right next door*.

My cell phone rang and I grabbed it from the windowsill over my sink, dove on it actually, relieved to have something else to think about besides Charlotte.

Unknown number.

All the people who called me called from unknown numbers, and when I called them that's how my number showed up. Because that's how people like us worked. With phones we could throw away. With people we would betray in a heartbeat if we had to.

Because all of us were unknown to each other. Fucking dark shapes in the darker lives we lived. And I'd gotten to a point where I didn't fucking care about it. Didn't care about who I'd become.

And then goddamned soft moved in.

"Yeah," I said into the phone.

"He's in." Sal, my boss, said back, and I felt an unparalelled spark. A wild fury. An adrenaline rush that got me hard.

"When?"

"Saturday. End of the month."

Two weeks away. "That'll work."

"He wants to go against you."

"That was the idea."

"Jesse, you know I don't argue with the way you run shit, but this guy...he's pretty real. And he's the tip of the iceberg. You say yes to this fight and hold your own, there's going to be a line of guys looking to fight you."

"That's the idea."

I could hear everything Sal wasn't saying. I could hear how he doubted I could fight and win against this guy, much less the lineup of even more legitimate guys that would come behind him. I could hear that he worried about me.

And I didn't need anyone worrying about me.

"You get some openers and I'll set it up," I said.

"Your brother isn't going to—"

I hung up and went into my bedroom to change into some new workout clothes. I'd call David, see if he wanted to spar. If he couldn't get us into his gym, I'd open up the basement.

In my bedroom, it occurred to me that my apartment was the exact same as Charlotte's. The layout, anyway. Open kitchen, tiny living area with the windows. Bathroom off the dark bedroom.

Even the bars were the same.

I had a king-size bed and a couch up against the wall in my bedroom for the shit I liked to do after a fight, and I had a TV in the living room with another couch against the wall. Otherwise I hadn't done shit to my place in the two years I'd been here. The walls were dingy. My curtains were old sheets.

She'd painted her walls yellow. The color of sunlight.

We had the same apartment, but hers was worlds away.

And it needed to stay that way.

CHAPTER FOUR

Charlotte

The fruit stand thing was this:

A few blocks from my old place on the corner of California and Powell, there was this organic fruit market and it was run by these brothers. Three of them. Maybe they weren't brothers, but for the purpose of my fantasy they were. I didn't know their names, but I had their personalities all mapped out.

The big guy, he was the boss. The brother in charge.

The middle brother, thin and elegant with a beard and the smile that cut right through it—he was the charmer. An almost pathological flirt. It didn't matter if a woman was young or old, skinny or fat—if she had a vagina, he flirted with her.

And the youngest brother, he was quiet. But a trouble-maker. He never weighed anything. Always charged people too little for what they were getting, and when Boss Brother called him out on it, he only shrugged.

Little brother didn't give a shit.

At first I went to this fruit market just for the fruit. They sold cheese, too, and some fancy meats, because that was the kind of neighborhood I lived in. And then I started noticing how hot they were. And then I couldn't stop noticing how hot they were. And I wasn't alone. The shop was full of women all the time—not just for the cheese, if you know what I mean. And I just imagined that these fruit stand guys got tons of action. Like all the action. Like maybe the fruit was just a coverup for some kind of hot fruit-related sex ring.

And then one day, middle brother called me *darling*. Actually, he said, "Can I get you anything else, darling?" and it was so loaded, his smile so suggestive, that he could really only be talking about one thing.

Of course I stammered and stuttered and looked anywhere but at him, said *no thank you*, despite wanting it, despite having dreamt about it, put my fingers between my legs imagining it, and I practically ran out of there.

But after that, all I could imagine was one day going in there and the fruit stand being empty. Just me and the brothers and the over-ripe peaches. And I would be wearing that summer dress I love, with the bodice that doesn't let me wear a bra, and I'd flip that Open sign to Closed and turn the lock on the door. And that lock would be so loud all the brothers would stop what they were doing and look at me.

"What are you doing?" Boss brother would ask, all grumbly and angry.

"I think I know what she's doing," Charming brother would say, and he'd be right, because he started this with that beard of his.

"Finally," Bad brother would say, and he'd just strip off his shirt.

After that it was a kind of...whatever I wanted hodge-podge of internet porn and romance novels until I got off.

The Fruit Stand fantasy had sustained me for years. It was a little secret shame, a gang bang fantasy I could never say out loud, I couldn't even look directly at.

It was a secret. My secret. Hot and private.

And my Bad Neighbor fantasy had the potential to be so much better.

Because I could make it real. Because it wasn't the hugely unlikely event of taking on three men in my sundress, it was just me flirting with my neighbor. And my neighbor flirting back.

I mean, I was no dating genius, I had no powerful understanding of men, but he'd been flirting. He'd indicated a certain amount of interest in me.

I just had to be bold, wild. Brave.

To put it bluntly—I had to be someone else entirely.

I had to be my sister.

The third day after Cheetara reached out to me, I was eating my lunch—Froot Loops with a side of baby carrots—and staring at that message request.

Three weeks ago, she came to my condo in the middle of the night, frantic and wild and so scared I thought she might vibrate out of her skin. She was so scared that when she told me she had to leave town, that she was in danger and she needed enough money to stay gone for a long time, I didn't hesitate—I called my real estate agent and told her I had to sell the condo. Fast.

Abby and I moved into a crappy hotel by the airport while we waited for the sale of the condo and all the paperwork to be finalized. Abby found me Shady Oaks by basically looking out our hotel room window, and when the condo sold we bought her a new car and off she went.

And I came here.

And it felt, right now, like I was missing a body part. That's how much I missed her.

But, still I hadn't accepted the friend request—because that would be crazy.

But I hadn't rejected it yet, either. Because I was lonely. And I missed my sister. And I really, really wanted her to tell me to go have crazy fruit-stand sex with my neighbor.

When we were kids and we'd played Thundercats, she'd been Cheetara because Cheetara was the only girl Thundercat, and my sister always liked being the only girl in the room.

I was Panthro. Because I was serious. And fixed shit.

Of course, the shit I fixed—it was hers. A life she broke and I put back together only so she could break it again.

My own life, I couldn't figure out.

Work, yes. In three days I'd finished the rough of Jane Austen in Hyde Park (I'd used the Serpentine Lakes). But in three days I hadn't left my apartment.

I was great at work.

Terrible at life.

So, I stared at that message request and had an imaginary one-sided conversation with my sister.

"I need a reason," I said out loud. "A reason to knock on his door."

No. You don't. You just need to go over there and make it clear you want to have sex with him.

I wiped the milk off my chin and counted the reasons why I couldn't just go over there and do what so many women my age were able to do.

"One: I am way too awkward for that shit. I mean... he's beautiful. I'm not exaggerating. Two: I'm probably thirty pounds overweight. And he's like the fittest person I've ever seen in real life. And third: my sex life has a real *Where's Waldo* vibe to it." (My sex life being Waldo).

"And finally, he's run hot and cold with me and yeah, maybe he was flirting but he's also been pretty insulting. It's not like I'm sure if I went over there and said *take off your clothes*, he'd say yes."

I said all that out loud.

He's a guy. He flirted. He'll say yes.

"Oh!" I said, lifting my dripping spoon in a Eureka moment. "I could break something in my apartment and have him come over and fix it."

Really? You want to be the damsel in distress. Again? You've done that twice.

"Good point." I mean, I was a damsel in some distress, but I didn't want to go around advertising that fact.

I needed to think of it as thanking him for fixing my stuff. Moving my things.

A thank you.

I dropped the baby carrot I was eating and sat up.

Perfect. A Thank you.

Sure, upon first meeting Jesse made me feel vaguely threatened and insulted. But since that meeting he'd been nothing but kind. And helpful. He fixed stuff. Moved my things. That was owed not just an apology, but perhaps a homemade dinner.

Guys liked homemade dinners, all the sitcoms said so. And I happened—thank you, Mom—to make a pretty great baked ziti.

And Jesse seemed like the kind of guy who would like a baked ziti. And a six pack of beer. I thought about baking a pie, but I couldn't bake pies and that seemed a little too eager to me.

"Thank you, Cheetara," I said, determined not to worry about my sanity.

I closed down Izzy. Got dressed and went to the grocery store.

While the ziti was cooling, I showered. Put some product in my hair, attempted to blow it dry, gave up and put it back in a bun with a backup headband. I put on my swishy blue skirt and the retro red shoes that made my legs look miles long. I wore my favorite pink v-neck shirt that those two people on *What Not To Wear* said would make me look thinner. I put on some mascara, a little lip gloss, and decided I looked pretty good.

Great, even. For me.

I wrapped the ziti in a dish towel so I wouldn't burn my hands and grabbed the six pack of some microbrew I'd never heard of and locked my apartment.

Outside, it was a purple twilight. The fog had burned off and the sunset was lighting up the sky in pink and orange. Pantone colors 213U and 021U.

The planes were overhead. But the planes were always overhead. It was why there was a vacancy and the rent was so cheap.

There were two women sitting in the lawn chairs by the empty pool, drinking what looked like juice glasses of red wine, and I realized it was Friday night. They were pretty, those women. One was white with red hair, the other was black, her hair in intricate braids. Both wore jeans with strategic holes in the knees and upper thighs and cute little sweaters to combat the chill of the early October evening. They looked like they might be my age—twenty-ish. Two twenty-ish-year-old women having a ladies' night by an empty pool.

It was the kind of thing that should be commonplace in my life, but somehow it was completely foreign.

They lifted their hands to me and it seemed like they might invite me over, and for a moment, I couldn't breathe with panic. Panic and a kind of wish. A wish that they would. A wish that I was the kind of person to accept if they did. But in the end they didn't, we just exchanged waves and I was left a little empty.

I took the two-step journey over to Jesse's door, feeling at once like I was about to have a moment that might change my life and a little like I might throw up in my mouth.

You can always hide your horn-dog motives behind being neighborly, I told myself and took some comfort in that.

I knocked on his door, but there was no answer. I knocked again, aware of those women behind me, undoubtedly watching.

Probably judging.

Maybe even laughing.

"Word to the wise," one of them yelled and I turned. Yep. They were laughing. "Stay away from 1A."

"I'm not...there's nothing—"

"Oh, he's fucking hot," the other girl said like I hadn't opened my mouth. "But he's bad news."

"Total asshole," the other woman agreed.

"We're just neighbors," I yelled with an inane laugh, and turned back to the door just as it opened and Jesse was standing there.

With his shirt off.

"What are you doing?" he asked. His eyes were definitely not sort of smiling now. They were hard and cold and I realized with a start that this was a mistake. A big mistake.

I went hard into bumbling mode.

"I just... this is... thank you. For fixing my stuff and...everything."

"What is it?" He tilted sideways like he was looking through my glass baking dish.

"Baked ziti and...here...beer." I held both out to him like I was carrying a dead cat. Like I'd been forced to do this. Like there was nothing more awful than bringing him food.

"I don't want that stuff."

"What?"

"I didn't ask for that stuff."

"Yeah, I know. That's why it's a gift."

"I don't need any fucking gifts."

Oh my god. This is so bad.

"Wow...okay." I was shocked speechless at his rudeness. He put his hands up on the top of the doorframe and leaned out toward me, every muscle in his body popping out in relief.

"I don't want that food, but that other thing you're here for. We could do that."

"Other thing...?" I was short-circuiting.

"Yeah."

"What—"

"Fucking. Right? That's why you're really here. To get fucked."

Oh my god. This was out of control. I practically incinerated on the spot.

"I don't...no...that's not—"

I mean it was, but I expected it to come after some conversation. A beer. Some smiling eyes. Not like this, with those women behind me and his cold expression in front of me.

"Bullshit," he said like I had disappointed him. "Take your food and get lost."

He shut the door in my face, and before I could move he opened his door again, grabbed one beer from the six pack I'd brought, and shut the door.

My blood was boiling. Literally boiling. While at the same time my skin was ice cold, frozen with a mortification so profound I couldn't think. Or breathe.

Leave, I told myself, my brain sending panicked and hurt messages to my body. *Move!*

On wooden legs I turned to back to my apartment.

"Don't take it personally," shouted my audience. "He's like that with everyone."

I didn't say anything. I didn't even acknowledge them. I went right back into my apartment and threw the ziti away. The beer I kept, planning on drinking all of it tonight.

I sat at my computer, because it was the only place I had to sit, and wished that my sister had not fallen in love and fucked up my life. But more than that, I wished she was here. I wished my sister was in the city and I could call her and tell her what just happened.

Because it hurt. It really hurt.

I opened up that friend request, hit accept and typed:

I need you...

I sat there waiting for a few hours, but my message went unanswered.

CHAPTER FIVE

Charlotte

Abby was born first. She was blue and small, her lungs under-developed. Immediately she was put in the care of a nurse. And the nurse had to put her in an incubator, where she stayed for three weeks.

I came out two minutes later. Pink and, while not fat, at least a better weight. I screamed and screamed and didn't stop until Mom had me at her breast.

"She's a hungry one," the doctor said, and that was pretty much when the jokes started.

That I, while in Mom's tummy, ate all the food. Leaving poor Abby to shrivel and wither and not develop her lungs. The jokes were so upsetting that at one point I went online and found all the information I could about how twins develop in the womb, but no one was much interested in it.

The jokes were so damn funny, who cared about biology?

But between my sister and I there was a different dynamic. She didn't laugh at the jokes, or tell them, and in thanks, I took care of her. I carried her extra inhaler and her EpiPen for a nut allergy she outgrew. I explained very carefully to all of our friends' parents that we couldn't come inside if there was a cat or a dog in the house. And even though I didn't have the allergy, if there was a cat and all its dander in our friend's house, I walked home with Abby.

I helped her at school. And Abby needed a lot of help. Or at least was very good at pretending she did.

I heard Mom one day telling her friends that sometimes she thought I was a much better mommy to Abby than she herself was. And I'd been fucking flush with pride. It was like she'd said the nicest thing in the world to me.

And then, as Abby got older and outgrew the inhalers and the braces and the allergies and instead started to grow into a kind of reckless wild boy-crazy walking hormone, I continued to try and mother her.

She called me—repeatedly—a drag. And that was exactly right.

I used all my weight to steady her. To counterbalance her whirlwind. I was hanging off of her, trying to slow her progress into the stratosphere.

That's who I'd become. And that's who I stayed.

A drag.

But without her in my life to lift me up, the only person I dragged down was myself.

Over the course of the next week, I licked my wounds by doing some of my best illustrations, my most clever lettering.

By never leaving my house.

I reminded myself that this was how I lived best. This was my happy place.

A little bit here, sure. In the world with the people I didn't like and who didn't know me.

But mostly I lived in my head. In my own world.

Working. Always working.

I was finishing up the last of the Newgate Prison pages by taking some liberties with the galleries, opening up a few of the cells in order to show how the female prisoners lived. The rank and foul and unfair conditions they had to survive.

Very chilling, if I did say so myself.

Yesterday sometime? Last night, maybe—I couldn't be sure when I was in this mode, time kind of became irrelevant —anyway, at some point I had scanned the illustrations and was tweaking the layout on my monitor when there popped a big red alert box on my screen, sent from my calendar program.

It's the last Saturday night of the month. You Know What That Means!

I clicked ignore, knowing even as I did it, it was futile. Five minutes later there was another one.

STOP! NOW! TAKE A SHOWER! PUT ON REAL CLOTHES!

I cursed my past self and this clever idea I had three months ago. There was no ignoring this anymore. My computer would start to shut down in ten minutes, so I saved all my files and shut everything down myself.

The last window I closed was the Facebook messenger.

Abby never responded.

And I'd convinced myself that the Cheetara thing must have been some kind of spammy prank. My sister would have responded by now. Abby did not have the impulse control NOT to respond.

With my computer off I had nothing to do but get ready for Torture Night. Or, as the rest of the world called it: A Pleasant Night Out With Friends.

Yes, I do have friends...well, acquaintances, really. A bunch of other illustrator/designers who got together once a month to commiserate and—in my case—practice rusty people skills.

I could tell myself some big story about how it was good to network and see what other people were working on and talk about the industry, but the truth was it forced me to put on slightly uncomfortable clothes and even more uncomfortable shoes and make conversation.

And as much as I might hate getting ready for it, I was always happy I went. If for no other reason than I left feeling like my work was always the most interesting work.

I'd rather work on *Where's Jane Austen* than winery labels for pinot noir. Or packaging for organic raw dog food.

And I needed to not feel the lingering burn of Jesse. In fact, I needed to clean Jesse out of my head. Two weeks in this place, and it felt like I was infested with him. Aware of him on the other side of my wall all the time.

So I put on my skinny jeans and my high-heel silver booties, that my sister made me buy a year ago, and a glittery tank top that covered up my belly and a fake leather jacket, and I let my hair down around my shoulders, in a big wild mess of curls.

And I painted my lips bright red. So you couldn't miss them.

You couldn't miss me.

And I felt good.

Really good.

Sexy even.

I stepped outside and turned to lock my door. Of course, because the world was cruel and ironic, Jesse, wearing a sweatshirt with the hood pulled up, was just walking into his apartment.

I kept my head down, my cheeks hot, and locked my door like he wasn't there. Grateful that my hair down around my face was such an effective curtain.

"Fuck. Charlotte?" he asked, and like I was a woman playing the part of a diva in one of those kinds of movies I flipped my hair (which was no easy feat) and walked away, strutting as best I could. Feeling his gaze on my ass the whole way.

———

Jesse

The fight was tonight. Everything was set up and for some reason, as I paced my apartment waiting for David to show up and tape my hands, all I could think about was Charlotte.

Not her ass in those jeans, which...I mean, fuck.

And her hair, the spiral curl cloud of it. And her lips, red like a warning flag.

No, I wasn't thinking of those things.

Instead I was obsessing on the too-short distance between her door and the door to the basement. The entrance to the fights was through the parking garage behind the apartment complex, and that door into Shady Oaks was locked, but if someone came up those stairs, they could unlock the door and be at Charlotte's door in two steps.

And the kinds of people that would go up those stairs from the fight...they didn't belong anywhere near Charlotte's door. Including me.

Especially me.

I grabbed my cell phone and called Nick. Not the woman who ran shit around here, but Nick who was one of the Downey boys. The Downey boys had their thumbs in all sorts of pies. Legal and not so legal. But Nick didn't quite fit the Downey brother mold.

He was a good guy. As far as good guys went in Shady Oaks.

"Hey Nick," I said when he answered.

"Who is this?" he asked, because my number had undoubtedly come up unknown caller.

"Jesse."

"Hey, man," he said. "Heard you got an event in the basement tonight."

"Full ticket. Should be good."

Good being an understatement.

"I'm wondering," I said, "if you might be looking for a little work."

"I told you, I'm not interested in fighting."

"Yeah, I know." Such a goddamn waste of a man built like a beast. "This is just a little security at the top of the stairs coming up into Shady Oaks."

"Outside your apartment? You've never had security there before."

"I haven't, but this new girl moved in. And if something happened, some drunk guy goes out the wrong door, she's the type to call the cops." Which wasn't a lie, but wasn't the reason why I wanted someone outside her door. "You know how this crowd gets."

Bloodlust being an understatement.

"It's two hours of work," I said. "And a good cause."

Nick laughed. "Good cause. Right."

He gave me his price, which I agreed to, and I gave him the time.

"Hey," he said just as we were about to hang up. "I know you and your brother don't talk. But he's sent out word that there's a girl he's looking for..."

"What else is new? Look, man, I don't give a shit about my brother's love life."

"Well, he says the girl he's looking for moved into Shady Oaks."

I rocked back on my heels. The fuck?

"It's not my neighbor," I said. "She's not the kind of woman Jack pays attention to."

The idea of Jack and Charlotte in the same room together was, frankly, funny. Charlotte would fall over herself and Jack would...well, he'd eat her alive.

"Yeah, just thought you might want to know."

I liked Nick. So I just barely managed to swallow my "fuck you, asshole, you have no idea what I want to know."

We hung up, and Dave arrived to tape me up, and I pushed Charlotte from my mind.

It was time to go to work.

————

Charlotte

All the designers met at one of the tapas places down in SoMa. Stephanie picked. Stephanie always picked. The rest of us introverts let Stephanie boss us around like it was her job, and I wasn't sure about everyone else, but I was alright with it.

It was enough just to be out in the world like this. The air smelled good down here, full of people and coffee and garlic. I liked the way my heels hit the sidewalk, and when I walked into the tapas place and was led by the hostess back to the table I liked how everyone stopped mid-conversation to say hello to me.

Like I was the thing they'd been waiting for. A missing part to a puzzle.

"Hey guys," I said, lifting my hand in an awkward wave. I liked the attention, I just didn't know what to do with it.

"Have a seat!" Stephanie said, pointing me toward the

empty eat at the end of the table. Right next to Simon, a fairly new guy to the group.

"I don't think I've ever seen you with your hair down," he said, after I sat down next to him.

"I don't usually," I said, abundantly aware of its size. My hair could, in some instances, be the biggest thing around for a city block. "It's kind of obscene."

"It's kind of amazing."

Well, that was charmingly done. And he looked sharp in his dark-rimmed glasses and fledgling beard.

Simon's elbow brushed mine and I felt it down my back.

Well, well, I thought. *Look at me now*.

I ordered the cheapest thing on the menu that wasn't nuts, and took a glass of wine from the bottle Simon ordered.

"Hey," he murmured as Stephanie started a conversation with Janice and Phil at the other end of the table. "I don't want this to be awkward," he said. "But Stephanie told me about your folks."

For a second I couldn't remember what I'd told Stephanie about my parents. But then I remembered how she had called during the first manic twelve hours after my sister told me the trouble she was in.

I turned my head so fast, my hair practically smacked him in the face.

"Sorry," I said.

"It's all right," he said with a gracious smile, straightening his glasses. "But I just wanted to say, I had to do the same thing a few years back. Dad had to go in for cancer treatment and insurance didn't cover it, so I sold my condo and moved into an apartment in Oakland. Gave them the money."

"Yeah," I said, lying through my teeth. The lie actually easier the more I told it. "It was a car accident. Both of them were in the car. They're fine, but it's lots of rehab. Insurance didn't cover it."

"That's tough. Where did you end up moving?"

"South San Fransisco, by the airport." His eyes widened and I shrugged. "Rent's cheap."

"Here's to cheap rent," he said and tipped his glass to mine. The crystal rang out with a cheerful sound. Convivial. Two people who understood a difficult truth sitting around a table of people who didn't.

Only I was lying.

My parents were doing just fine in a condo outside of Miami.

They didn't know I'd sold my condo and given the money to my sister so she could go underground. My parents lived a very separate life than me and Abby. It had always been that way. They were a unit, and me and Abby were a unit. We joined up every few holidays, but that was it.

"Anyway," Simon said, "I'm going to need your help finishing this bottle."

Oh, God. It was so kind. He didn't want me to be embarrassed by not having any money, but he still wanted me to relax and have a few drinks.

"I don't believe that for a minute."

"Share it with me anyway," he said, his shoulder bumping mine. I waited for a zing or some kind of internal alarm. The kind that happened around the fruit guys.

And Jesse.

No zing, just a kind of...awareness. Of a person so close to my space. I didn't hate it, but I didn't crave it either. I didn't feel electrocuted by his skin. But he was attractive in the same way I was attractive. Unnoticeable initially. Quirky, if you liked us. Flawed, if you didn't.

We matched.

Jesse and I were worlds apart. We didn't even make sense. I wouldn't know what to do with him and he wouldn't know what to do with me.

Across the table, Stephanie waggled her eyebrows at me and I realized this was a setup, and I didn't even have it in me to be irritated.

I blushed but managed not to tilt my head forward so I could hide behind my hair. "I would love some wine, thank you."

It briefly occurred to me that I could probably break Simon over my knee if I had to, that's how much smaller he was than me. And of course as soon as I had that thought I was sure I would have a glass of wine too many and actually say it.

Which was how my social anxiety worked. But Simon was a good talker and we discussed work for a while before our food showed up.

What I ordered happened to be a giant plate of potatoes, which were more than delicious. Especially washed down with Simon's wine.

Jesse who? I thought as I flipped my hair and attempted my best flirt.

And it must have worked, because outside of the restaurant after Stephanie and everyone had filed off into their Ubers, he asked if he could call me.

"Anytime," I said.

"No." He was blushing, which was sweet. "For a date. Can I call you for dinner or drinks or something?"

"For a date! Yes. Yes. Of course. That would be...lovely." Lovely sounded lame, even to my ears.

But in the cab ride home he called—not texted, called.

"Sorry," he said. "I couldn't wait. Want to meet for coffee next week?"

"How about next Wednesday?"

"You tell me where."

And because the only coffee place I knew was my old afternoon iced coffee hookup, I gave him that address.

"It's a date."

A date. I hung up my phone and pressed it to my chest.

I had a date.

The cab dropped me off in front of the crappy half-stucco wall that separated the majestic paradise that was Shady Oaks (note the sarcasm) from the relative squalor of the neighborhood, and I felt a little bit like Cinderella after the ball, rolling up in my pumpkin coach to my bed of ashes.

"Really?" my driver asked, taking in my glittery shirt and rocking boots. "You live here?"

"Home sweet home," I said. I thought of Simon and the people around that table eating octopus and drinking Campari and sodas like they were water, talking about theater and restaurants and work. I would get back there. I would. This was just a...speed bump. A minor setback.

This was not my life. This place. Jesse. Not for me.

My advance check would come in the mail soon and I'd be gone.

And all of this would be a memory.

I paid the cab driver and walked through the rusted gate into the courtyard. The edge of the pool was a relative party tonight. A few guys were sitting in folding chairs, and all of them looked similar. Brothers, I thought.

The black girl who'd witnessed my scene with Jesse was there. Everyone turned when I stepped up.

"Hey! It's 1B!" they cried. "Come have a drink."

"I've already had a few," I said.

"Perfect," one of the men replied. "So have we."

"Thanks, but I'm for bed."

I stepped past the pool toward the shadowy corner where my apartment was when I heard someone from the pool jogging to catch up with me. It was the girl from the other day.

"Hey," she said. "I really hope we didn't embarrass you the other day."

"No, that was—" *already taken care of by Jesse*. "Nothing."

"Look, I know you're new here and you keep to yourself, but someone probably should have told you. He's really trouble."

"Yeah, I've gathered."

"And whatever shit he's running in the basement. Just..."

"What's he running in the basement?"

She glanced back behind her at the group and then leaned forward. "I heard it was illegal gambling."

"Jesse?" With the frayed shorts and the tool kit? That didn't seem to fit.

"Whatever it is," she said, "just... stay clear."

Something about this woman's good intentions pissed me off. I didn't need anyone telling me how to live my life, but I thanked her anyway and continued back into my shadowy corner of the world.

It was dark so I didn't see the guy standing outside the basement door until I was practically on top of him.

"Jesus!" I screamed.

The guy took one long look at me. My sparkle and my hair. My shoes.

"Entrance is in the parking garage."

"Entrance for what?" I asked, edging toward my door.

"Oh, you live in 1B?" he asked. "Charlotte?"

"How the hell do you know my name?"

"Jesse told me."

"Jesse? Who the hell are you?"

"Security," the guy said. My eyes adjusted and I finally soaked in the details of him.

Dude was big. In all possible ways.

He wore a black tee shirt and a black leather jacket over it.

I didn't have to be told that he probably had a gun under that jacket.

"Security for what?" I asked. My back against my door. I was trying to get my key in without looking. It wasn't working.

Big man held up his hands as if to show me he had no weapons. "Consider me security for you," he said.

I heard the sounds of people and music coming through the door behind him.

The door that said: *Basement. Keep Out.*

The door Jesse made me promise to stay away from.

"What's going on down there?" I asked.

"I mean this with all due respect. But what's going on down there's got nothing to do with you."

What the fuck with people tonight?

"I could just go down to the parking garage, couldn't I? Find out for myself."

"Yep," he said with a nod. "You could. Or you could go into your apartment. Make yourself some cocoa and just rest easy knowing I'm standing here and I'm on your side."

"I don't drink cocoa."

"Okay, you could do a bowl of heroin and call it a night."

"I don't do heroin either," I said with a laugh, which made him smile, a flash of white teeth in the darkness.

"Well," he said, "I figure most of us are somewhere in the middle."

"You're really here for me?"

"I'm here to make sure no one comes up those steps."

"And Jesse—"

"Hired me to be here. Yep."

Oh, that shouldn't matter. That shouldn't do anything to me. Shouldn't make anything ping or get hot or feel good.

I looked through the open archway to the patch of grass and the low-rise parking garage in the distance. I could go find out what was happening in that basement, but what would be the point?

This wasn't my world. I was only visiting.

"What's your name?" I asked the security guy.

"Nick."

"Thanks, Nick. I hope no one comes up the stairs."

And I went into my apartment and shut the door on this world.

CHAPTER SIX

Charlotte

I was having a sex dream. With Neil Patrick Harris. It was full of mixed messages.

But I woke up with a start when there was a loud, hard thud against my door.

Nick. I thought, my heart in my throat. Someone must have come up the stairs.

I fumbled for my glasses and put them on so I could see the clock. It was five a.m. I nearly screamed when there was another *thunk*.

I scooted out of bed, pulling down the men's flannel shirt I was wearing to sleep in, and I ran to my door to peep through my peephole. All I saw was the back of someone's head.

And the sound of a key going into my lock.

"Hey, Jesse," a woman said. "Your key doesn't fit."

"This isn't his door," I yelled through the door, but the sounds of the key scraping at my lock didn't stop. So I undid my chain, my bolt, and then my lock, and pulled open the door only to have Jesse and a black woman stumble into my apartment.

The woman barely caught Jesse before he was on the ground.

"Sorry," she said, and I had an impression of a beauty like a knife. Sharp features and dark eyes, but I barely paid attention.

Jesse had been beaten. Badly.

He was bleeding. Big drops fell in splatters on the white tile of my floor. I wasn't sure where he was bleeding from, because he wouldn't lift his head. His hands curled up against his chest were both raw and swollen. Fixed into fists.

"Oh my god," I said, and grabbed a dishtowel and put it under water. "What happened?"

He lifted his head at the sound of my voice and I pressed the cold dishtowel to his face. His nose was where the blood was coming from. His eyes were dark purple with bruising.

Pantone color: 19-3218.

"Sorry," he murmured. "Mistake."

"I'll say," I said.

"Great," the woman said. "You got him. You did great tonight, Jesse. But you're no fucking good to me like this. Later."

She put his key into my hand and vanished. Just vanished. Leaving me at five o'clock in the morning with a pummelled Jesse.

"I just need you to open my door," he said, lifting his swollen hands. "I can't..."

"Of course," I said, made more panicky by his calm. Like this was no big deal. A thing that always happened to him. "Can you walk?" He was leaning against my doorframe, and I held my hands out wide like I would catch him, or carry him if I had to.

I couldn't. There was no way I could, but there was no telling my adrenaline that.

"I can walk," he mumbled through his beautiful split lips. But he wasn't too steady on his feet. A problem he solved by keeping one shoulder against the wall, dragging himself against the building to his door. The wall was stucco and I winced, imagining how that hurt. But maybe he was so hurt that little thing didn't even register.

"Sorry," he mumbled. "For bothering you."

"It's okay, Jesse."

"It's not."

My hands were shaking and it took me a second to get the door open. But once it swung open, he lurched inside, swallowed by his dark apartment.

He left the door open and I still had his key in my hand.

I could set that key down on his counter and just close the door behind me when I left. Or...

The sun was coming up, the violet sky turning mauve along the edges, and I looked at the round edge of the sun just visible over the parking garage in the distance and thought about concussions. And that actress who hit her head and everyone thought was fine but then she died. And I thought of his hands, so bruised they were useless.

It wasn't like I really had a choice. Not if I was a compassionate human. I simply couldn't let him be here alone, so I went inside the apartment, closing the door behind me.

I found him in his bathroom, fumbling with a bottle of extra strength Motrin.

"Here," I said, quietly into the hush of his bathroom. "Let me."

"Go home," he said.

Ignoring him, I took the bottle from him and shook out two pills, thought about it and added a third, and then put them in his ruined hands. He swallowed them dry.

"You should go to the hospital, Jesse."

"Why?"

"You could have a concussion."

"I could."

"And you don't think the hospital will help you?"

"I either have a concussion or I don't."

He was saying it like it didn't matter, and I realized I had my hands pressed to my chest because it hurt me to see him so hurt.

"What can I do for you?" I asked.

"Go home."

"I'm not going to just leave you here."

"I want you to leave me here."

"That's probably just the traumatic brain injury speaking."

His ruined mouth gave the impression of a smirk and he stepped toward me, which was so weirdly shocking that I jumped out of the bathroom. He stumbled across the hall into what had to be his bedroom.

In the dark I heard the springs of his bed catch his weight. I went into the kitchen and opened his freezer, hoping for a few icepacks, and found a freezer stacked with frozen blue pouches.

I took out a few but couldn't find any dishtowels to wrap them in, so I carried them—so cold they hurt my hands— into the bedroom.

His bedroom was dark, but the slice of light from the hallway cut across his body where he was lying on the bed, his feet still on the floor, staring at the shadows on the ceiling. He wore his workout clothes again. A gray shirt and a pair of ratty shorts. On the leg of the shorts it said in very faded red and yellow lettering: Iowa State.

Iowa State like the University?

"Jesse," I said. "I have some ice packs..."

He rolled his head toward me and again, even half obliterated by swelling and bruising, I could feel his gaze. The heavy weight of it. Like a hand against my skin. "Where do you want them?"

I saw that he wanted to tell me to leave. The message was in his body. It was something he exuded. *Leave me alone*, every muscle and tendon and bruise and blood smear shouted. But I stood in the doorway and I didn't listen. Because he was hurt. He was hurt so bad.

Finally, he sighed, exhaling so deeply his body deflated further into his bed.

"My hands," he murmured, lifting his fists and setting them down again against his chest.

I put one on each of his hands. He hissed and then sighed like it felt good. "Do you want one on your face?" He nodded. "I couldn't find a towel or anything. You should wrap it so it doesn't hurt. A tee shirt or something..."

"Charlotte," he said, again so calm. So quiet. "Everything already hurts."

I nodded like that made sense and placed one of the squishy blue icepacks over his nose, covering his eyes. He hissed again and then sighed.

"Thank you."

"You're welcome."

In the silence I could hear him breathe. I could smell his sweat.

"What happened to you?"

"I got the shit kicked out of me."

His dry tone startled a laugh out of me. "Did you call the cops?"

He shook his head, dislodging the ice pack, and I put it back into place. I was standing awkwardly over him, aware with every breath of the scent of him coming up out of his sheets. Something warm and manly, but also blood. And sweat.

The smell of a man and something gone a little wrong.

"No cops."

"Don't you think you should?" I asked. "Call the cops?"

"No. I don't. Go on back to your apartment," he said, all prickly again. "I'll be fine."

I shot him a completely incredulous look that he couldn't see. Because there was no part of him that looked like he would be fine. Not without serious medical help.

"You're acting like this happens to you all the time," I said, shifting one of the ice packs on his hand, tucking it a little into the hole between his thumb and fingers. Finally I gave in to the inevitable and I sat down on the bed next to him, and it was like sitting down next to a fire. I was careful, so careful not to touch him but it didn't matter. He burned so hot I was scorched anyway.

"How do you know it doesn't?"

I thought of his bruises on the day we met. His broken nose.

Clearly he fought. A lot. Like... I mean, it seemed ridiculous, but my whole life had sort of turned into the ridiculous lately—but was this his job? "I don't think you usually get the shit kicked out of you."

"Feels like it."

"Is that...in the basement...is it some kind of...one of those fight club things?"

"No."

"Why are you lying?"

"Why are you pretending you care?" he shot back and I blinked at him, startled he had the energy to be so angry. And then... I realized he didn't. He wasn't angry. Not really. He could barely hold on to his scowl—he just didn't want me asking questions.

And I didn't want to look too hard at why I cared.

"How does the other guy look?" I asked, reaching forward to shift the icepack to a better spot over his eyes.

Again, that shadow of a laugh. The slight grimace of a smile.

"He's not conscious."

"I take it that means you won?"

"Doesn't it look like it?" he asked and I laughed, surprised he could still be cracking jokes when he had to be feeling like road kill.

"Did you at least make some money?" I asked. "That's how those things work, right? You nearly die but you make a bunch of money?"

"How would you know how those things work?"

"Television tells me how most things work."

His chest lifted again in a weird hurmphy laugh. Without defenses, he found me slightly entertaining. It was a strange thing to realize.

"Yeah. I made a lot of money. More than I've ever made before."

"You do this a lot then?"

"This is all I've ever done," he said. "This is what I know how to do. It's what I'm good at."

The bluntness of his words. The bleakness of them...made me so sad for him. What he was good at was violence? Was some kind of fight thing in a basement? A job that left him like this—beaten and alone in his crappy apartment?

"You can fuck yourself with that pity."

I started, shocked at the pointed anger in his tone.

He was staring at me, his dark eyes under the ice pack, illuminated by the light from the hallway. "I'm not... it's not."

"It is. And I don't need that fucking pity. Not from you."

"What does that mean?" Not from me. Like my pity was more abhorrent than anyone else's.

He sighed. "Nothing. It means nothing. Go away. Seriously, I'm beat to shit and I'm not in the mood to be worried over." Still lying on his back he began to toe off his shoes, but they were stuck and so I reached down and yanked them off.

"What are you doing?" he asked.

"Yeah, I'm real sorry I'm not the kind of person who can just...leave you like this." I thought of the woman who just left him with me, like she couldn't get rid of him fast enough. I threw his shoes into a dark corner of the room. "You're hurt. And I get it, you're a super tough guy, but you shouldn't be alone right now."

He was watching me underneath the ice pack.

"You have bumblebee curtains."

"Yes I do," I snapped. "And you have..." I looked at his window. "Oh come on. A sheet? Are you a college freshman?"

He laughed. "No. They keep out the light, what else do I need?"

"I don't know, something you don't hang with duct tape? I hope you're going to take a bunch of that money you won and buy yourself some curtains..."

His silence was the kind I had to fill.

"So, I have very cute bumblebee curtains and you have a sheet over your windows and ...what? That's why you don't like me?"

"I never said I didn't like you."

"Really," I laughed. "Because that is not how it feels on my end."

"I like you just fine," he said. "But those curtains tell me everything I need to know about you."

"Oh, this should be good."

"You're soft, Charlotte. You're part real, part dream. You're half here and half...someplace else."

He'd blown a hole through me. Right through me. He was right. Completely right and it wasn't like he was the first person to tell me I lived most of my life in my head. But it was that he had seen that. In the ten minutes we'd spent with each other he'd seen the truth of me so clearly.

"All that from curtains?" I said, reaching for a joke.

"And your hair. You don't belong in Shady Oaks, babe. It's way too hard for you."

"You don't know me, Jesse." I said it, not as protest, not as some flip line trying to prove something to him. It was just the truth. He didn't know me. I didn't know him.

He sighed, and upstairs something thunked and there was a muffled voice. Two people in conversation. The world waking up. Pretty soon the sun would come through that sheet and the day would be starting.

"Where'd you go tonight?" he asked and I blinked in surprise. "All dressed up. Date?"

"No. No date. Though...I got asked on one."

"Yeah? Who?"

"You think you might know him?"

He scoffed in his throat. "I know I don't know him. I'm just wondering what kind of guy you go on dates with?"

"He's a designer. A friend. He's nice."

Jesse winced. "Nice? Nice sounds like a shitty date."

"You like to date assholes?" I thought of the woman who dumped Jesse on me.

"I don't date anyone, but 'nice' sounds like shitty sex."

"Shitty...what?" I cried. This conversation had gone around a sharp corner.

"Sounds like missionary under the covers. Lights off."

That was how I liked my sex, but I wasn't saying that. At all.

"You looked good, tonight," he said.

"Don't—" I said before I could stop myself.

"Don't what?"

"Lie."

"I'm not lying. You know you looked good. You strutted away from me like you were fucking Beyonce."

The compliment was making a mess of me. And that it was from him was almost devastating.

"Fine. Then don't be nice. It's confusing. It's easier when you're an asshole."

"Easier not to like me?"

"Oh, no, not liking you is pretty easy."

"Easier not to want to fuck me, then."

I was stunned into silence. Nothing was going to make me not want to fuck him. He was the fruit stand guys times ten. A potent fantasy I could not have, because having it would ruin it.

I would ruin it.

"Your hair," he said and reached up, the ice pack falling off his fist, to touch one of my curls where it hung off my shoulder. I was suddenly aware of how short my flannel shirt was, and I wasn't wearing a bra. And we were on his bed. And the darkness was thick and hushed. Insulation between us and the world.

This was happening. It could happen. I could kiss his busted-up face. But even as I thought that, even as I wanted it—I rejected it. Because that was what I was good at.

Rejecting what I wanted.

"You want a drink of water?" I asked, getting to my feet. Hot and prickly. Wanting to stay in his bedroom and wanting to get out at the same time. "I'll get you a drink of water."

I stood up and went into the kitchen to get a glass of water. To get a breath.

His cupboards had two glasses, two plates. Two bowls. In his cutlery drawer there were two forks and two spoons. His fridge had Gatorade and eggs. A package of roast beef sandwich meat.

It was the loneliest thing I'd ever seen.

"You should have come in the other night," he said and I jumped, shutting his fridge door. He was standing in the doorway outside his bathroom. He'd taken off his shirt, and his chest and ribs were red and raw. Like he'd been rolled over gravel.

"Looking at your fridge, you should have taken the ziti," I shot back, and to my astonishment his lip curled in a smile like he liked me giving him shit.

"You shouldn't be up," I said.

"Motrin kicked in. I'm fine." It was such a lie and still he walked closer, tossing the thawing ice packs into the sink. Stepping closer still until I was wedged up against the fridge.

"Stop," I finally said, putting my hand up, a breath away from touching his chest. So close I could feel the heat of him against my palm. So close I could imagine how he would feel.

Good. He would feel so damn good.

Solid and real when so much of my life was not.

"You don't want me to stop," he said and pressed forward up against my hand. "And you don't want fucking nice. Not you. Not now."

I bit my lip, swallowing the gasp in my throat. He was so hot. Burning against my skin. He was soft. Silky. The muscle a strong curve beneath my hand. I wanted to sink my nails into him, but his body had been brutalized enough.

"You can't... you're hurt," I said, fumbling and gasping. He stepped closer again, his stomach touching mine. His leg brushing my knee and I felt like a fever had spread from his body to mine.

This felt like a dream. Or a movie. Nothing about this was real.

"Not too hurt to fuck you," he said. "It would feel so good. So damn soft. Your skin. Your hair. I bet your pussy is so fucking soft." One of his hands slipped up under the edge of my flannel shirt and brushed my thigh and then, with his hand, with his whole hand he grabbed my ass. And squeezed. It hurt so good my knees buckled. He held me up with his body and I could feel his cock against my hip. Hard and blunt. I was wet immediately. So turned on it hurt.

"You feel it, don't you?" he whispered into my hair. I made some half-gasping *what* sound in my throat. "Empty. So empty where I'm going fuck you."

Oh God. Oh my God. Yes. Yes, I was empty. I was so empty I was hollow. My head was so heavy, it fell back and hit the fridge. I could barely keep my eyes open.

He squeezed my ass again, his leg bumping into mine, not an accident this time, a nudge and like I knew what he wanted, like we shared the same mind I stepped wider, letting his leg in between mine. His thigh, bare beneath the cloth of his shorts, pushed up against my pussy. My underwear a thin nothing between us.

"Baby," he groaned. "Baby, you're wet. You're wet for me already."

Baby. I'd never been anyone's baby during sex. During anything. And I fucking liked it. I loved it. I loved it so much I got even wetter. And I wasn't even embarrassed. There was no room in me for embarrassment. I was filled with a liquid heat and a painful desire that pushed every other thought away.

"You want to know how I would fuck you?" he asked. "If you dressed up for me like that?"

I nodded, just barely. Just enough.

"I'd bend you over this counter. And I'd spank this fucking ass. Nice isn't going to do that to you."

My ass. He was talking about *my* ass. Squeezing it in his hands like he couldn't get enough of it. Like he needed more. And I'd never been spanked, couldn't even imagine wanting that—but this moment, right now, I wanted it more than I'd wanted anything.

Too much. This was all too much. I didn't know what to do with my hands. My body was falling apart inside my skin. My heart and lungs weren't working. My brain was screaming *run*, but my legs didn't remember how to, so instead I pushed down against his thigh, so hard. And he was right. I was wet and I was empty and I wished I was the kind of woman who could say *fill me. Just fucking fill me. Now.*

With your cock. And your fingers and your tongue.

Just fill me until I don't feel empty anymore.

His other hand slipped under my shirt and I almost missed it but he winced. As the bottom of my shirt grazed over the broken skin of his knuckles, he winced. Just that tiny touch hurt him.

"Your hand," I gasped.

"Forget it." He pushed his thigh harder into me and I could have come. I could have ground myself down on him a few times and I would have come. And he hadn't kissed me. Barely touched me.

Barely knew me.

And I barely liked him.

"Stop," I said. The words coming to my lips so much easier. So much faster than *please fuck me*. He didn't stop, he settled his body harder against me and I could see the bruises forming under his skin and I didn't understand why he was doing this. Or why he would want to. And I realized with a kind of breathless cold calm, that this wasn't really about me.

This was about him. And the fight. And not wanting me here. Not wanting me to care.

"Stop, Jesse. Please."

And just like that he stepped back, his hand leaving my ass to settle momentarily against my waist as if making sure I wasn't going to fall down. I twitched away from him, away from the fridge to the middle of the floor.

His erection pushed out against his shorts, and he

reached down and arranged himself and it was kind of the hottest thing I'd ever seen. I wanted, suddenly and with mouth-watering force, to watch him masturbate. I wanted to see those muscles in his stomach coil. And his hand grip his cock. I wanted to watch him bite his lip and come on his chest.

"Jesus," he muttered. "Why are you stopping? Look at you, you want it so fucking bad."

"Look at you," I said quietly, because he was right, I did want it so fucking bad, but his hands were a mess and his face was even worse and I could see what his body would look like tomorrow. "Jesse, this has to be hurting you."

"I'm not worried about it, why are you?"

This felt so off, so strange. "Why...? Do you want me to hurt you?"

"No," he said. "I've been hurt enough. I want to feel good. And you feel so fucking good."

Oh. God. I had to put a hand up against the fridge. Make a show of straightening my glasses because I couldn't look at him like this. I didn't know how to want something like this. The degree to which I wanted to make him feel good was quickly making a mess of me.

"Go," he said, his voice hard and mean. "Just get the fuck out of here."

I blinked. Stunned. He was scowling at me like I was such a disappointment. How did he go from stroking his cock to kicking me out in a nanosecond?

"You're not stopping because of me," he said. "Not really. And I got no time for a girl who can't take what she wants. See you, 1B."

And then he turned and limped out of the room, leaving me alone in his kitchen, feeling like a fool.

Again.

CHAPTER SEVEN

Charlotte

It was strange living next door to a man I wanted to avoid, but the walls between us were so thin I knew, nearly all the time, what he was doing.

He argued with the ten o'clock news and then watched *The Daily Show* before bed. Trevor Noah made him laugh, and the sound of it was a dark rumble through the plaster and paint between us.

He had a weird affinity for country music. And rap music. Those two and nothing in between. It was sad songs about dogs and lost loves, or it was wild songs about sex and rough neighborhoods.

Every other morning he woke up at six a.m.—an ungodly hour—and went running. He ran for one hour, coming back by seven to play music and jump around his apartment. Working out in some capacity, I gathered. The other days he ran in the evenings. Same hour. No jumping around afterwards.

My life, in a way, grew attuned to his. He woke me up in the morning and I couldn't go to sleep at night until he turned off that TV and went to his own bedroom. The loud ding of his microwave reminded me it was time to eat, and the sound of his door opening and shutting as he went for his various workouts, forced me—out of sheer guilt—to stand up. Move my body. At least to the coffee pot and back.

I hated the guy, but we were like symbiotic creatures in a way. I was the bird in his hippo mouth... or something.

There was no ignoring him.

———

The next few days passed in a blur of work. I stopped to sleep and that was about it. I ate at my computer. I canceled my date with Simon, because I couldn't muster up the energy to make small talk about the lie I'd told about my mom and dad. After that I wasn't sure what day it was, much less what time it was when the phone rang and I barely looked up from my layout to answer it. I pressed speaker so I didn't have to stop working.

"Hello?"

"Charlotte?"

"Speaking."

"This is Emily, at Bloom Books."

Jesus. Right. My editor. I stopped working and picked up the phone.

"Hi, sorry, I'm just working on a layout."

"Well, I like to hear that," Emily said. "I'm actually calling because of the last images you sent."

I winced in preparation. "The prison pages? Too much, huh?"

"No! No, not at all," she said, rushing to assure me, and I

leaned back in my chair. "I'm calling because they are amazing. The entire office is buzzing about this book."

"Well, that's super nice to hear."

"We would like to tour you."

"Tour me?"

"Put you out on a book tour. August and September for the release."

"What does that mean?"

"Well, you'd be traveling for two months to major cities, where you'd do some signings and maybe some events—"

"Events?"

"Talk to people."

Oh, this was sounding worse and worse. And something in my silence must have broadcast my feelings.

"It's a very special book," Emily said.

"I think so too," I said. "I just...I'm not really a people person. The events—"

"We don't have to do events. We'll just do the signings. We can make this whatever you want to make it. But we think a tour will really help the book do well. That's all we want."

I wanted that too. Who didn't want that? But all I could think about was... all those people. And two months away from home. From work. Izzy.

What if my sister called? Or reached out? I needed to be here for her. In case something went wrong and she had to run. Again.

Even as I thought those excuses, I knew how lame they were. Facebook was on my fucking phone. And she would call me, not show up at this apartment building she didn't know I was living in.

But those lies were so much easier than the truth.

Which was—I was scared. I was scared to leave. I was

scared to meet new people. Talk about my work. Put myself out there like that.

I was too fucking scared to try.

"Just...think about it," Emily said. "We can make it as easy for you as possible."

That seemed unlikely.

"Okay," I said. "I will think about it."

And mostly I would think: no way.

And I would hate myself.

———

Before I knew it, it was Saturday again and I hadn't seen Jesse once in the last week. Heard him plenty, thought about him far too much. But had managed to do my laundry at night and avoid him entirely when I left to go grocery shopping.

But Saturday morning rolled around and all I could think about was Jesse down in that basement, fighting again. I didn't know that he would be there, couldn't imagine his body would feel good enough to do it.

But not much about Jesse made sense to me.

My body was tuned to sounds on the other side of the wall, but it was quiet on his side. Like maybe he wasn't even there.

Throughout the whole of the day there was not even the bing of the microwave when he ate his Hot Pockets, or whatever it was he microwaved with such regularity. I imagined him like a barely grown teenage boy—not true, obviously, but I took comfort in the small, petty things.

I kept looking out my peephole for signs of Nick, but the basement doorway stayed empty. And from next door there was no sound. I went so far as putting my ear against the wall before I realized I was being an idiot.

Finally after dinner, I heard his door open and the murmur of voices. Another man and a woman, and soon he turned on his music—not the rap or the country, but something with a sexy bassline and a woman's voice—and I breathed a sigh of relief.

There wasn't going to be a fight. Or it didn't feel like there would be.

So, I shook off my worry and opened a bottle of wine.

And got out the Brie and crackers.

When it wasn't the last Saturday of the month, this was My Saturday Night Tradition. I called it date night, and thought it was hilarious. And since it was date night and the rules of date night were no work, I put on the BBC *North and South* miniseries and called watching Richard Armitage research.

Armitage was just scowling at Daniela Denby-Ashe when the porn started next door.

At first Jesse just turned up his music. Way too loud. I checked my watch—ten o'clock—and scowled at the wall I shared with Jesse. Rude much?

And then the thumping started. The rhythmic thumping.

That's not…I turned down the speaker on my computer.

And I heard the moaning.

Thrust. Moan. Thrust. Moan.

Oh my God.

I pulled my legs off my desk with a thunk.

He was having sex with someone next door. I turned up *North and South,* and even that wasn't enough. I plugged in my ear buds and finished off my bottle of wine and tried with all of my might not to think about Jesse having sex with someone.

I wasn't hurt. Or wounded.

I mean I was a little, but mostly, if the bottle of wine I'd just put away could be honest for me: I was turned on.

What was he doing in there? What was he doing that was making the woman—screaming now—feel so good?

Here's the truth—there wasn't a whole lot of screaming in my sex life. Not that lights-out missionary position didn't have its finer moments, but they usually didn't involve screaming.

I would bend you over this counter.

Before I realized what I was going to do I'd turned down my monitor so I could hear it better. It wasn't just the woman screaming now, I could hear the rough bass of Jesse's voice. It was sharp, like he was yelling at her. Ordering her around.

I would spank this ass.

Between my legs I hurt—and I'd spent the last week wearing out the batteries on my vibrator, masturbating to images of Jesse doing all the things to my body that I didn't even realize I wanted, and my hand was halfway down my pants before I realized I was about to masturbate to the sound of him having sex with another woman.

Too much. Too far. Too weird-neighbor. Too *get your own fucking sex life*.

Too goddamn sad.

The whole scene was sad. The Brie and the crackers. The empty wine bottle.

Enough.

I cleaned up, ignoring both the soundtrack next door and the aching throb between my legs.

Finally, there was a big shout and a woman screamed and I did a slow clap and crawled into bed.

Only to be woken up an hour later by round two.

Jesus, I thought, staring up at my ceiling and the lights from the parking garage outside my window. *What kind of stamina does Jesse have?*

By three a.m., I was livid. And when it started up again after a brief respite, I put my glasses back on and stormed over to Jesse's door. I was sleep-deprived, half-drunk, half-hungover and I'd had enough.

I didn't consider what I was going to say or do. I didn't consider what Jesse's face would look like. I didn't consider any of it. I was just mad. I had work to do. And he was rubbing this shit in my face. It felt weirdly personal. A show he was putting on to show me what a coward I was.

Of course that could be the wine talking.

I pounded on the door, aware that behind me half the apartment complex was asleep, and when no one came to the door I pounded again.

Harder. So I could be heard over the endless sex happening, and finally it was wrenched open, revealing a beautiful black woman who looked vaguely familiar, wearing a thin jersey tank top and nothing else. She was flushed, her long hair sweaty and stuck to her neck.

Her dark eyes raked my body and then she smiled. "Fun," she said. "Come on in."

"Do you have any idea what time it is?" I yelled over the sounds of the music.

"Nope," she shouted back and turned and walked back into the living room, turning left toward the bedroom.

And I stood there like an idiot. Was I supposed to follow? Did I want to follow? I heard the low rumble of what had to be Jesse's voice, and I knew if I went back there I couldn't lie to myself anymore. I could be outraged—and I was, but If I went back there it was because I wanted what was happening back there. Because, if nothing else, I wanted to see it.

I was mad, yes.

But underneath it, like my anger was a suit of armor keeping me safe, I just wanted to *see it*.

I wanted to be the girl, the type of girl who went back there.

And so I put my apartment keys on the edge of his kitchen counter and I did.

CHAPTER EIGHT

Charlotte

There was a man sitting on the edge of the king-size bed, and between his legs was the woman from the door. She'd taken off her shirt and was kneeling on the floor. The man's cock in her hand.

All the air got sucked out of my body, the room, perhaps the world, and as I watched, the woman slowly slipped the head of his dick in her mouth. And the man—I assumed it was Jesse—wrapped his hand around the back of the girl's head and fucked up and into her.

His head was down as he watched her take him, but I realized belatedly that the guy was blond. And thin.

Jesse was neither of those things.

Panicked, I looked around and found Jesse sitting on the couch on the far side of the room, watching me watch them.

His eyes glittered in the dark.

The dim light from the kitchen made its way across his body. His chest was bare, the bruises from last week in brilliant Technicolor. Sweat was rolling across the muscles. His collarbones. I tried not to look, I did, but in the end I couldn't help myself, I glanced down at his crotch but it was shadowed and I couldn't tell if he was naked.

I couldn't tell if he was hard.

I felt like a teenager, blind and dumb with hormones.

"What are you doing here, 1B?"

"Your music is too loud."

Like my answer was the wrong one, he turned and watched the couple. The guy was lifting the woman's hair out of the way, while she licked him from his balls to the tip of his cock. Long slow licks, leaving him wet. The gleam of her saliva was golden in the half-light from the hall.

"Look at me," the man breathed, and the woman on her knees did as he asked. Holding his cock with one hand as she put his cock back into her mouth.

They were so beautiful, the two of them. Each of them long and thin, muscular but not like Jesse. They looked like porn stars. The room smelled like sweat and sex and it was the hottest thing I'd ever been a part of, and all I was doing was standing in the doorway.

"What are you doing here, 1B?" Jesse asked again.

"It's...it's three a.m.," I said, my voice breathy and wretched.

Jesse turned away again, watching the couple on his bed.

"Suck him," Jesse said. "1B wants to watch."

I gasped, my eyes back on Jesse like he'd betrayed me.

"You do, don't you?" he asked. "Or maybe you want to pretend you don't. Pretending is easier for you, isn't it?"

It stung, it stung deep and hard where a lot of my secret stuff lived. The things I didn't like to acknowledge about myself. The things that kept my life so small. So small it felt like a jail. The fucking book tour. Simon. Jesse. Wanting more, taking less.

I didn't say anything to Jesse, but I stood in the doorway and I watched the people on the bed.

And I didn't leave. It was hard. It was a fucking force of will. But I didn't leave. Because I did want to watch.

The girl smiled at me and then bent her head to the guy's cock. His hand in her hair tightened and she took him deep.

"All the way," Jesse said, like he was orchestrating this whole thing. And maybe he was. Maybe we were all just puppets.

And the girl took the man as deep as she could, until her face was pressed into the hair at the base of his cock. So deep and so hard that I thought for sure she would pass out. Or stop breathing. The man held her there. Fucking into her. Forcing her to take more.

I was about to say stop—that there was no way that she could want that—when she sat back with a sudden gasp, her face split into a smile, spit hanging from her mouth.

The man wiped it off with his hand.

"1B is worried you don't like that," Jesse said.

"Like what?" the girl asked, her eyes dilated, her face blissed out.

"Tell her," Jesse said to me, but I didn't. I couldn't. Participating somehow would mean that I was really here.

I shook my head, barely. But Jesse knew.

"She's scared you don't like sucking cock like that," Jesse said. "She thinks we're forcing you to do something you don't want."

The girl's eyes found me. "I like it," she said. "Do you want to try?"

My legs buckled and I fell back against the door, making it bang against the wall.

At the sound the guy turned to look at me, too.

"You all right?" the blond guy asked.

"Fine," I said with a smile, like we were at the grocery

store and I wasn't watching him get his dick sucked. "Go back...to...that."

"You like to watch?" the girl asked. "Or do you want to join us?"

"I...uh..." Oh, this wasn't hot anymore. This was just awkward, and I was so totally out of place with my flannel shirt and my socks and my hair back in a bun.

I was wearing fucking glasses. Who wears glasses to your neighbor's orgy?

"Don't talk to 1B," Jesse said. Like he knew I wanted to run. Like he understood I could watch but I could not stand to be the focus of anything. I would crumble under that.

The girl rolled her eyes at me, as if somehow we were sharing a private joke about Jesse being bossy, but then she put the blond's cock in her mouth again, taking him all the way into her mouth. Down her throat. The man got in on it, holding her still, holding her tight against him.

"Deeper," he whispered to the woman. "You can do it. You can. You're so fucking hot. So good, baby. Sucking my dick like that. All the way."

She made some sound of despair or desire, something that blended the two and she braced her hands against the bed and finally leaned back, the spit this time between her lips and his cock like they were connected.

She went back. Again and again.

It was the most brutal and amazing thing I'd ever seen. The consent. And the...desire. On both their parts. His restraint and her enthusiasm.

The grace of their surrender to each other.

I leaned back against the door, panting. I could barely shut my mouth and my nipples underneath my flannel shirt were so hard. Painfully hard. Between my legs...I hurt. I hurt so bad.

The wine was making a mess of me.

My loneliness was making it worse.

It was like watching something I never knew I wanted. Like finding out there were other flavors of ice cream. Secrets rooms in all my favorite places.

This, I thought, is what the bold get to have.

"Charlotte," Jesse said and like I was dazed, I looked at him. Unable to hide anything I was feeling. I didn't even know how I would.

And his flushed face. His bright eyes. In the shadows between his legs his hand was slowly moving. The other two people on the bed. The blowjob. Everything, all of it —disappeared.

It was me and Jesse. And nothing else.

"Come sit down." His voice was quiet. Beseeching almost, like he wanted to convince me to stay. Like it mattered to him. "I won't touch you. Not if you don't want me to. But we can...we can watch together."

On the bed, the guy was groaning. The woman's hand around his cock, stroking now. Faster and then faster still.

"Or," Jesse said, "you can leave. And go back to your half-here, half-somewhere else life. And you can pretend this was a dream. We'll avoid each other in the courtyard and this can just disappear."

That is exactly what I would do if I left.

And it seemed, all at once, so empty. So cowardly. He wasn't forcing me to do anything I didn't want to do. He was forcing me to do what I *wanted*.

He was putting this gift in my hands.

I crossed the room and sat down on the couch beside him. Careful not to touch him because that would make all of this feel too real. But the couch was small and I had the sensation of him all along my leg. My side. My body vibrated with the nearness of him.

The air tasted salty and tangy, like we were all just breathing in sex. I was so turned on I thought I might combust. Shifting on the couch, my thighs squeezed my clit and it was all I could do not to do it again and again. Right here, in front of people.

Out of the corner of my eye I could see Jesse's hand on his cock, but he wasn't hard.

I actually started at the sight of his semi-hard dick. How in the world could he be sitting there, watching these beautiful people, telling them what to do, breathing this air—and not be turned on?

"I'm tired," he said, like I'd asked the question out loud, or maybe my staring at his cock just made my thoughts so freaking obvious. He was smirking at me, his ruined mouth pulled tight at one corner. And I couldn't stop myself from imagining him having sex with that woman, her sleek body and his sleek body. I imagined his hands in her hair.

Her mouth on his body. His cock... I made some strangled noise before staring back at the bed.

"Ask me," he said, his voice low, thick. Humid even.

"What?"

"Whatever you want."

"Did you fuck her?"

"I did."

"Did you fuck him?"

"Would that bother you?"

I couldn't answer. I couldn't even breathe. I pressed my legs together, squeezing my clit. The idea so exciting. So outrageous I couldn't think past the idea.

"I didn't," he said. "Not tonight."

From this position I couldn't see much, the girl's back, the man's hand in her hair. The bob of her head. The gurgle in her throat.

But it was no longer the hottest thing in the room. Sitting

in the dark next to Jesse, it was breathlessly intimate. My entire body was tuned to him.

"You want them to do something else?" he asked.

"Is that...how it works? You tell them what to do?"

He shrugged.

"Like live porn?"

"Like a bunch of deviants who get their rocks off fucking each other," Jesse said. He turned to the couple on the bed. "Matt, go down on Amber."

"No," the blond guy said. Gasped really. He looked like he was about to come.

"Charlotte wants to see it."

Matt gave Jesse the finger and kept sliding in and out of Amber's mouth.

"Sometimes it works," Jesse said. "Sometimes it doesn't."

"Please." The word croaked out of me before I even knew I'd been thinking it.

Everyone turned to stare at me. Amber over her shoulder, her lips red from being stretched around Matt's cock.

I didn't look at Jesse, but I could feel him watching me.

And I loved it. Not a little. A lot.

I loved all of this.

"I would...like to see that."

"I guess I wouldn't mind either," Amber said with a wink and got up off her knees. She lay down on the bed and Matt took her spot on the floor, kneeling between her legs. Again, I couldn't see much. Amber's legs stretched to accommodate Matt's broad back. But I could tell when Matt licked her, Amber jumped. Sighed and then put her fingers in his hair to push him closer.

"Look at you," Jesse said, still watching me. I got the impression those two on the bed could burst into flames and he wouldn't so much as glance away from me. "So brave."

Not looking at him I opened my mouth to say something.

To tell him to fuck off, or stop staring or something, but nothing came out. My breath shuddered in my body and I wanted to touch myself so bad I could taste it in my throat.

"Touch yourself," Jesse said and I flinched, his words turning up the desire in my body even higher. Even hotter.

I would die here like this.

But still I didn't do it.

"Let me touch you," he said.

And "yes" gasped out of me.

He made some low humming noise in his throat and I closed my eyes braced for his touch.

Stupid me. Like I could prepare for something like Jesse's touch. It was like being shocked by electricity. Like stepping naked into the wind. It was only his hand on my upper thigh, pushing the hem of my sleep shirt up, but I jumped. I nearly screamed.

I closed my eyes and bit my lip.

"No," he said. "Look at me."

"Jesse," I breathed. "No."

"You can do it, baby, open your eyes." I felt the fingers of his other hand against the side of my face, barely there and yet all I could feel. His fingertips were rough and callused and I flinched, but succumbed to his pressure, turning my face until I felt the back of the couch against my cheek.

I waited, holding my breath for his fingers to slip under the lace edge of my underwear, but they didn't. His breath was so loud in my ears, the gust of it warm against my lips.

I licked my lips and he groaned and the sound pulled my eyes open, like I had no control.

And there he was. His beaten-up face, his tender mouth, curled in a half smile. Whatever I was expecting to see on his face, the smirk or distance, a teasing whatever... it wasn't there.

"You are so fucking beautiful," he murmured and before I

could cringe away from the compliment, his fingers found me, over the silk of my underwear. He was so sure, so fast. His touch so heavy and so right that all I could do was gasp and spread my legs.

Slouched in the corner of the couch, I let him touch me. His fingers all over me. Pushing past the thick seam of my pussy until he had the wet silk of my underwear pushed up against my clit.

"Is this how you like it?" he asked and the question was so oddly kind. So...chivalrous when I expected him to go full Neanderthal on me that I shook my head. Honesty getting the best of me.

"Inside," I breathed.

And his fingers slipped under the silk, over my belly and speared, right into the heart of me.

I cried out, bowing off the couch, my hand holding his hand against me. "Yes," I cried and then, like he was a tool for me to use, I ground myself against him.

Blood was rushing in my ears and I watched as Amber on the bed started to coil up and jerk against Matt's mouth. And I realized in some crazy half-present part of my brain that I was going to come at the same time as this woman I was watching have sex.

How. Was. This. Possible?

"Come on." Jesse's breath against my shoulder was hot and damp and I wanted his breath on my whole body. I wanted to throw myself up to every dark and depraved experience I could get in this room.

"Charlotte?" Like I had lost all will, he said my name and I looked at him. And kept looking at him, aware of his smile. Of his hand. Of my body. The air and the world.

And when I came—the great wild shattering thrill of it tore me apart. Scattered me around the room. Left me broken on that couch. His hand between my legs. My eyes still locked on his. I was crying out. Gasping.

"Jesse!" I cried and he touched me again, making my body jerk over and over until I could take no more. Until I pushed him away.

My brain was wiped clean. All that shit I worried about, that kept me locked down. That kept me scared. Alone. It was gone. The relief of that, of this moment of total freedom from the reality of being...me, made me laugh.

Made me want to cry.

And then, as I watched, as it seemed like every bit of pleasure and feeling had been wrung out of my body, he lifted his hand, the hand that had been between my legs, and licked his fingers.

And I was ready to go again. It was like I hadn't just come. Like I had never come.

I wanted to fuck everybody.

On the bed, Amber was coming, I recognized her screams from the ones I heard earlier through my wall, and when she lay replete on the bed, Matt stood up, his cock unaffected by gravity.

"Fuck," he groaned. He touched himself and looked my way. "You want to?"

"No," I said, at the same time Jesse said, "No."

I glanced over at him and found him watching me. "I'm not sharing you. You want to come again, it'll be me doing it."

That should not excite me. It should horrify me. But everything was upside down and inside out right now, and those words were the sexiest thing any man had ever said to me. By miles.

Amber, looking like she'd run a marathon, mascara running down her face, sat up from the bed. "Me," she murmured to Matt. "I'll take care of you."

Matt stepped up to her and like they'd done this a thousand times, like it was old hat, she opened her mouth and took him inside. Amber was weak and boneless and he held her head, easing himself in and out of her—using her until he came. Swearing and jerking and clutching her to him.

And it should have seemed ugly. Or strange. But somehow it was tender. It was that graceful surrender on both their parts.

And then... it was over.

And we were just a bunch of strangers breathing hard in a room that smelled like sex.

At some point in the last lifetime the music had stopped.

I felt sticky and damp.

Hungover now, more than drunk.

I wanted a shower. Some water.

All my boldness was gone and I pushed my shirt down as we all sat there, strangers having done a strange thing. Well, they might not be strangers, but I was. And this whole thing was beyond surreal. It was like an out-of-body experience.

I got to my feet. "I have to go," I stammered, not looking at anyone. Particularly not Jesse beside me.

"I'll walk you," Jesse said as I headed for the door.

"You don't have to." I didn't want him to. I wanted to go back to my apartment and recalibrate.

"Goodbye, Charlotte," Matt said, waving at me as he put on his underwear. Amber toodled her fingers at me, silent on the bed.

"Be gone when I get back," Jesse said to the two, who nodded without offense, like this was standard.

I practically raced out of there, snagging my keys from the corner of the counter where I'd left them before walking back into that room and changing my entire life.

Jesse's door was partially open—I'd forgotten to shut it when I came in, and I cringed thinking about who might have seen or heard me like that. I cringed about all of it. Buyer's remorse setting in hard.

"Hey," Jesse said, catching up with me at my door as my fingers fumbled with my key and lock. I was shaking. Adrenaline maybe, the desire and lust still in my body. I had no idea. I felt like I could run a marathon or fall on the floor and cry.

Or most likely, get in some kind of yelling match with Jesse.

"Charlotte," he said, putting his hand on my hand and I nearly smacked him away. "Let me."

"Don't—"

"You're shaking."

"I'm fine."

He was behind me. His arm stretched out along mine. I could feel him. Hot and big, standing behind me, and I closed my eyes in surrender as he took the keys from me. Slowly, he unlocked my door, pushing it open with my hand and I charged through with all the grace of an elephant.

I took great care to hang my keys up on their little hook. That really mattered right now, making sure my keys were over that hook. Just so. Just...right.

"Are you okay?" he asked.

"Great!" I cried in a painful Tony the Tiger Frosted Flakes voice. Internally, I winced. Internally, I wanted to die.

"Charlotte," he sighed and then he was behind me. My hands pressed to the wall, my eyes on that key and his body behind me.

He wore underwear, or shorts and nothing else. His bare chest, still damp from sweat, pressed into my back, making the shirt I wore wet.

My breath shuddered in and then stopped. My body shaking and hot and trembling and wretched and awful.

And ready. So ready for him. I was hollow again and only he could fill me.

"You want more." His breath ruffled my hair, burned across the back of my neck.

I did. I did want more.

"Let me give it to you." His hands cupped my waist, one sliding down my body to my hip, the other up to cup my breast, loose under the shirt.

"I knew it," he breathed. "I knew you'd be so fucking soft."

My head fell back, balanced resting against his shoulder, and for a moment it felt like he pressed a kiss to my ear. My cheek. Soft things, so unlike him. But then I stopped feeling anything but his hand between my legs, petting me over the damp ruined silk of my underwear. Petting me until I pushed into him.

He sighed at my eagerness, a rough low growl in the back of his throat like I had pleased him with that tame shift of my hips. And the need, the sudden fire deep in my womb to do exactly that—to please him—was lit. A tiny flame, but it was there. A need I couldn't wish away.

I would like to please him.

"I couldn't believe it when you walked into my room," he was saying, his long callused finger running over me, over and over again. "And you stayed. Did you like it?"

I couldn't answer, or rather didn't, and he stopped touching me, forcing me to whimper low in my throat.

"Answer me," he said.

"Yes. I liked it."

"What did you like the best?" He was stroking me again. His hand under my panties now, his fingers inside me and I shuddered against him. "Charlotte," he breathed. "Answer me or I'll stop."

"You," I cried out. "I like you the best. When you told them what to do and made me come. I liked you the best."

"Fuck." He tilted his head, finding the bare skin of my shoulder where my shirt had slipped out of place and he sucked my skin hard into his mouth. Hard enough that I thought he was biting me. Hard enough I didn't want him to stop.

Hard enough that I fell apart in his hands. Shaking and crying. My legs giving out so completely he pushed me up against the wall, holding me there with his body.

His cock was hard against my ass and I pushed back against him. An animal kind of welcome. An awkward overture.

But instead of lifting my shirt and plowing into me he turned me around to face him. Oh, his face, so bruised, it broke me and I moaned.

His fingers touched the mark he left on my shoulder. Half hickey, half bite.

"I like that on you," he murmured. "My mark."

"That's…I'm…"

He grinned at me and I stopped trying to make words, content to just stand against the wall, my inner thighs slick with my own come, my body a broken set of pieces, barely functioning as a whole.

I couldn't have predicted it but he slowly, carefully leaned forward and pressed his ruined lips to mine. So tender. So soft. I felt the split in the corner. His fat bottom lip was chapped and he breathed against me, tasting of mint and something musky.

My come. From when he licked his fingers.

I should have been revolted. I should have jerked back and pushed him away. But I didn't. I leaned back against my wall, the key hook digging into my hair and I let him kiss me.

I let his breath wash over me the same way I let him put his mark on me.

A willing victim.

"My favorite part was you," he said against my lips, as if putting the words into my mouth so I could have them to live on. To feed me when I was hungry.

And then he was gone.

CHAPTER NINE

Jesse

In the seconds between waking up and opening my eyes, I had the vague sensation of being...happy. I think it was happy. Happy was so long ago in my life, such a faraway thing, that I wasn't sure if I recognized it right.

Like looking at a shoe and thinking it was chair.

I was supposed to go running. Meet David down in the basement. Call Sal and make plans for the next fight. I had shit to do. But I didn't get up to do any of it.

Instead, I lay there and just let myself feel like I had something to look forward to, like there was something good waiting for me when I opened my eyes. God, when was the last time I felt like this? Those first months of school before everything went to shit? When I was a kid? In the house on Burl?

I didn't even know. I couldn't find this feeling in my past. This heavy contentment in my body with the wild soaring emptiness of my brain. Thoughts clicked over and over, memories from last night. Like in a movie.

Charlotte.

Fucking Charlotte.

Last night was real. It wasn't one of my fever dreams after listening to her putter around her apartment all day straining my ears so I could hear her hum.

It happened.

And I couldn't take it away.

And just like that—the second I put her name to this feeling, it was like I poisoned it.

Stop man, I told myself. *You didn't do anything wrong. You haven't fucked anything up.*

But it was too late. I tried to keep the dread away, the worry, but it was a cancer in my life, something I carried with me everywhere I went. Because I ruined shit. Things came to me—pristine and perfect—and I smeared them with my grubby careless hands.

I scrubbed my hand over my face and wondered how I was going to fix this. Because it couldn't happen again. She had no business getting this close to the shit I did in the basement. Not only was it dangerous, it was pretty fucking illegal. And if she had any sense at all she would have gotten the clue after that kiss in my apartment after the fight. Of course, if I had any sense at all I would have told her to leave last night. But she'd shown up like some kind of fucking horny good girl, bent on turning my world upside down.

And I couldn't resist her. Which, according to my brother, had always been my problem. All the discipline in the world when it came to fighting and wrestling—none at all when it came to the good girls I shouldn't touch.

Jesus.

She'd come so sweet. So fine. And we'd barely even started. I'd barely even touched her.

Under the sheets my cock twitched and got hard. Harder still. As I tried not to think about her on that couch beside me, watching Amber and Matt, telling them what to do. Watching her watch them, watching her get over being so scared, I'd never seen anything so hot. So powerful.

And I felt—a little—like I gave it to her. Like I was happy not just that I got to see it, but that I got to have it happen for her.

In a million years I never would have expected her to do that. Or again, in her apartment after, so agitated, so torn up, so ready to come once I touched her...

I could spend the next year making that woman come and it wouldn't be enough.

And I shouldn't do it again.

Next door, Charlotte's alarm clock buzzed and I ignored my dick and opened my eyes. She would hit snooze three times before actually turning it off, and I liked imagining her burying her head under the pillow, one hand sneaking out of the sheets to bang that alarm clock until it stopped buzzing. And this morning I felt like sleeping in with her, separated by that shitty wall.

So, I forced myself to get up. It was a gray South San Fransisco day, I could tell by the milky light coming in through my sheet.

Charlotte was right, I probably should change the curtains. But changing that was like admitting that this was my home. That I wasn't going to be leaving anytime soon.

That I had nowhere else to go.

Despite the years I'd been here, I was clinging to the fact that this wouldn't be my life...forever.

I needed a few more wins like last week's. A few more purses like that and I'd be out of this place. Out of this life. All debts paid.

And then what?

What happens when you get out of the hole you live in?

I flipped the blankets off and got to my feet. Kicking the sheets I'd torn off the bed last night after coming back to my apartment from Charlotte's, into the corner. I needed to do laundry. I checked in with my body. My ribs. My hands. The pressure in my nose. Behind my eyes. Everything still hurt, but it was time to get back at it. Training waited for no man. Right now my next opponent was probably running take-downs in a gym somewhere.

Thunder cracked outside and the world got a little darker as a storm roared in. Running in the rain used to make me feel like Rocky. Like some crazy man on a mission.

Now it just made me feel wet and cold, like a dog left outside too long.

I pulled on my shorts and walked into my kitchen, wondering if I had any coffee. It had been a long night and I was pretty much fucked out of any energy.

"Well, look who finally decided to get out of bed!"

I jumped and yelled and bashed into the door of my bedroom I was so fucking startled.

"Sorry," said the guy sitting on my living room couch. Sitting there like he had the fucking right. And for a second, the sleeping part of my brain, the boy I'd been, the little brother I still was—that part of me was so fucking *happy*.

I couldn't stop it. I couldn't change it. I had to let the happiness run through me like an electric current, followed almost immediately by the grief.

Maybe this was the dread I'd been feeling. Maybe my brain knew he was near, picked up on his menace. His fucking cloud of doom.

"Jesus," I muttered, "how the fuck did you get in?"

The man on my couch shrugged and got to his feet. I stepped back out of habit. Out of self-preservation. He'd handed down beatings in my life that made last week look like a party.

"How do you think?" he asked.

I didn't even have to look at my door to know he'd broken in. A habit he'd picked up when we were kids, and he'd honed it in the last few years.

"What are you doing here, Jack?" I asked, not wanting to think about when we were kids.

"Guy can't visit his brother?"

"You can visit anytime. You just don't."

Jack looked at me with Mom's eyes, blue as the fucking sky. And sad like Mom's eyes, too.

"Don't," I said.

"Don't what?"

"Look at me like you miss me."

I missed him like I missed my parents. Like I missed the life I was supposed to have. But two years ago that asshole walked away, and when I tried to follow he shut the door in my face.

So no. He didn't get to miss me.

He blinked and the sadness was gone. I remembered when Dad died, the two of us standing next to his grave as they lowered the cheap pine box into the ground. On the far edge of the cemetery had been the guys in the black coats, smoking cigarettes and watching us. Like vultures, waiting for our weakness to be revealed so they could gobble us up.

Don't show them anything, Jack had said in my ear. *Not now. Not ever.*

He'd gotten real good at not showing anyone anything.

I noticed for a guy who should be as broke as I was, he was dressed up pretty nice. He had a slick leather jacket and boots that looked like they cost as much as my rent.

He could have been any kind of guy standing there—

college kid, actor, a guy who worked down on the wharf. Anyone. Dark jeans. Gray shirt. Leather coat.

But the tattoos gave him away. I could only see the ones on his hands, but that was plenty. His arms were covered, sleeves of ink. He liked Biblical shit, no doubt from a childhood spent on his knees begging for forgiveness at St. Pat's on the corner of our old block. So his arms were like stained glass windows in church. Lots of blood and swords and lions and men casting brutal judgement and weeping women clutching babies to their chests.

It was beautiful and terrifying.

He was a bad man. And he couldn't hide it. Couldn't blend in.

And this is why Charlotte and I couldn't happen again.

Because I was this man's brother.

It literally sent a chill through me, thinking of her being in this room with him. It made me nervous that she was next door, the wall too flimsy when it came to my badass brother.

"I heard about the fight," he said. He ran a hand through his hair. His hair was longer than mine and curly, the way mine would be if I grew it out. When he was a kid rocking that long curly hair, waiters and waitresses always thought he was a little girl, but he didn't care.

He fucking loved that hair.

"You heard I won, then?"

"Yeah," he said, getting angry. I'd kill him now, if he tried. He'd gotten soft doing whatever the fuck he'd been doing for the last two years, and I had never in my life been so strong. "I heard you won. And next week you're going up against Martinez?"

I shrugged. Word got around.

"Out of all the things you could do with your life. You pick this?"

"This is making me a lot of money."

"Yeah," he scoffed, looking around my place. "I can tell."

"I'm good," I said. "I'm really fucking good."

He looked me over and I knew what he saw. My body was a machine. A weapon. All boyhood beaten out of it.

I was a man.

And I was a beast.

"Of course you are," he said with a sigh that sounded like our mother's when she caught us fighting. "But going up against these guys, you're gonna get killed. Or hurt for real. Remember Lars?"

"Of course I remember Lars." He'd been a neighbor on Burl. A grown-up man living in his parents' basement, playing video games with us because of something that happened to him in the war.

"Yeah, well, you're probably one concussion away from Lars. Tell me, what was the point of getting you free of all Dad's shit if you're only going to get yourself killed in some junkyard fight in a basement?"

"It's not like that."

"Oh, it's exactly like that."

"Well, it's none of your fucking business."

"You could have been anything—"

I went to door, ignoring the chain he'd cut through. My busted lock. I'd fix it all later. Just like I'd put myself back together, too.

"Don't rewrite the past, Jack," I said. "You were the one with the future, and you made your choices. I was born to be exactly this and we both know it. You should go. I'm sure you've got important shit to do."

"You kicking me out?" he asked.

I shrugged.

Jack sniffed, that tattooed hand rubbing over his face like I flat wore him out.

"I got another question," he said.

"I'm about done answering them."

"Anyone new move in here lately? A girl?"

"Why?"

"Why do you think?"

"Shady Oaks is a long way to go for pussy."

"It's not...it's not like that. I'm looking for a girl. A woman." I didn't so much as blink at him. There was no possible way he was looking for my Charlotte. It was like the big bad wolf looking for Little Bo Peep—they didn't belong in the same world. "The woman I want split. I don't know where, I'm pretty sure why, and I just...I need to find her."

"And you think she's here?"

"No, but I think her sister is here."

For some reason that made my heart stop. I was not a guy who believed in coincidences.

"Why?"

"I know they were staying in a hotel out by the airport up until a few weeks ago. I know the sister sold her condo and gave the cash to Abby. I know Abby paid cash for a shitbox pick-up and left town. But the sister... she stayed. And since she didn't have a lot of cash left, she needed a place with cheap rent."

"And you think it's here?"

"Lotta people hide out here." He gave me a pointed look.

"I don't pay a whole lot of attention," I said. "People move in and out of this place all the time."

"Yeah. Well, if you see anyone new or hear about some kind of artist—"

"Artist?" I asked, before I could stop myself.

Jack turned on me like a bloodhound. "You heard something?"

"No, I'm just...what kind of artist would move here?"

"One trying to hide." He stepped toward me and I could see under his jacket the outline of his gun.

Fuck, Jack. No. Don't tell me you're in so far you're never going to get out.

I looked away, wishing I could unsee it. He stopped an arm's length away from me. I could feel him looking at my face, taking in the old scars. The new wounds. "You don't have to do this," he breathed. "I can give you enough money—"

"What about Dad's debt?" I asked. I asked this question even though I knew the answer. I really knew the answer, low down in my stomach where I hurt every damn day. Where the pain lived that I couldn't fight or fuck away. "How are you going to give me money when we're supposed to be taking care of the money he owes to Lazarus? Last week I made back a chunk of it, you can take it to him. It's not all of it, but it's some." It was barely a drop in the bucket, Dad owed a fucking life-destroying amount of money and my purse was big, but it wasn't that big.

"Stop, Jesse," Jack said, his hand on my shoulder. I tried not to feel it but it was impossible not to. "Dad's debt's been paid."

"How—" I swallowed the rest of the question, because I knew.

The answer was in the tattoos on his arms and the gun under his jacket.

Jack paid back the debt in trade.

My heart just fucking broke. It broke in a thousand pieces.

Me and my brother—the people we'd been. Gone.

This was my brother, right here. Right in front of me. But he was an ice cold stranger.

"Mom wouldn't want you fighting like this," he said.

I laughed. "Yeah, you think she'd want you doing whatever the fuck it is you're doing with that gun under your jacket?"

His face got hard, mean. It was like seeing someone you loved put on a mask. Him, but not him.

"Mom's dead," he said for absolutely no good reason.

"I'm so glad she can't see who we are now," I said.

Jack blinked and looked away. But he was nodding too.

We would break her heart.

"Listen, you hear of a girl moving in, you let me know," Jack said. "It's important. Real...important."

I closed the door behind my brother and rested my head against the wall. I lifted my skull and pounded it back down for good measure.

Never. I would never tell Jack about Charlotte, especially if she was the girl he was looking for.

But other people knew Jack was on the lookout for an artist moving in here, and sure there was plenty of turnover in these apartments, but not a whole lot of single girls moving in all the time.

And an artist.

Jesus.

My brother was a stone-cold killer, and I had to make sure he wasn't looking for my neighbor.

CHAPTER TEN

Charlotte

My shower was as hot as I could take it. My skin alive with the pleasure-pain of the heat and the surprising water pressure. But good things didn't last forever at Shady Oaks, least of all the hot water, and as it drifted into cold I cranked off the water and stepped out of the old claw foot tub. My wet hair falling down my back, tame for the time being with water weight, I reached forward and swiped my hand across the mirror, clearing a stripe of condensation away.

And there was my face. The same as it ever was. Pale. Freckled. Bright blue eyes. Transparent eyelashes.

My sturdy body. The broad shoulders my mom always thought meant I was going to be a swimmer, such a disappointment for her.

The same as it ever was.

But there at the junction of my neck and my shoulder was the purple mark Jesse had left on me. I touched it with trembling fingers, but it just felt like my skin. It just felt like me.

It really happened. The proof was right there.

And instead of being embarrassed, I was amazed at how fucking proud I was of myself. Not because I'd done something dirty and kinky and was now ready for a life of group sex. But because there'd been something I wanted. Something wild and different and difficult.

And I did it.

Who is the drag now, huh? Not me.

And Jesse...God, how strange the gratitude was. How awkwardly it pulsed inside of me. A light I had no idea how to turn on or off.

It was Sunday, and for the first time in so long, work held no interest. I made my coffee and sat down out of sheer habit. Turning on my system out of muscle memory.

My designs appeared on the screen and I just...didn't want to.

I opened up my Facebook page and looked through the pictures I had with my sister. Lingering on the one from our last birthday. We were wearing boas and tiaras—she looked like she was born wearing them. I looked self-conscious. But she had her arm around my neck and her lips pressed hard to my cheek and we looked equally happy.

No one had been starved or denied. No one left behind.

It was us. And it was enough.

I clicked on the picture and made it my desktop picture. Replacing the sunset that had come with the system.

And then I decided I needed breakfast. Diner breakfast. Home fries and bacon. Endless cups of mediocre coffee. I grabbed my keys from the hook... pausing for a moment, my body frozen by the memory of Jesse's fingers inside of me.

That happened. That really happened.

When I opened my door, Jesse was standing there, his fist raised like he'd been about to knock.

Startled, I stepped back and he dropped his hand.

And for a second, naked and honest, we just sort of grinned at each other. Or I grinned at him and he sort of gave me the impression of grinning, and it was enough to make me blush. Enough to make me erupt in a full body blush, my body alive with memory.

And then he coughed into his hand, breaking eye contact, and his face, when he looked back at me was set into stern lines.

I wondered briefly why he did that. If I had a habit of pushing away the things I wanted, he had a habit of pretending not to feel anything, when he so clearly did.

"I'm going to go to Jim's," I said, naming the rundown diner a few blocks away. "Want to come?"

"No," he said and I blinked, the giddy/happy thing happening in my chest dissolving away.

"Okay," I said slowly. "Why are you here?"

"I just..." He glanced sideways down the side of the building, as if checking to see if anyone was watching and I was reminded, so clearly, so terribly of the time Chris Anthenet, the high school quarterback, asked me out on a date. He'd done the same thing, made sure no one was around to see him asking out Abby's fatter, shyer sister. "I can make you breakfast," he said.

"You don't want to be seen in public with me?" I asked and then was completely astounded that I did. Where had that come from? I was wearing my favorite sundress, the fabric printed with smiley-face suns, with my cowboy boots. My hair in a thick damp braid down the back of the denim jacket I'd thrown on.

I wasn't anything to be ashamed of.

"No!" he said with the kind of wide-eye surprise I couldn't imagine him faking. "I just don't...like people."

"Well, I can relate to that."

"I want to see you, and you're hungry. So, I can feed you."

I can feed you. How primal that sounded.

"What exactly will you make? Gatorade with a side of ice-pack?"

That made him really smile and I saw the white gleam of his teeth, the wrinkles at the corners of his eyes. He really was handsome. So handsome my stomach fluttered and I put my hand against it.

"Give me a half hour," he said. "And I'll be back."

"Not here!" I said, "I don't have any chairs, remember?"

He glanced around my apartment over my shoulder and then he nodded. "Right. My place, a half hour. You bring coffee."

A half hour later I was standing outside his door, holding a bodum of hot fresh coffee like a bouquet of flowers.

Weird. This is so weird.

I knocked, and his muffled voice answered, "Come on in."

The inside of Jesse's apartment smelled like a diner, the air thick with bacon and potato smells.

His table was set with his two plates and two forks.

This felt strangely like a date, between two people who knew nothing about each other and didn't like people. It felt like a date that didn't stand a chance.

"Hi," he said, looking up from whatever he was stirring on the stove. He wore workout stuff again. It was not hard to imagine that was all he wore. Like he didn't have other clothes.

"Hi," I said.

The awkwardness was excruciating. It was actually painful. What in the world would we talk about? What could we talk about? Group sex? Unexpected voyeurism? I wanted to walk across the room and kiss him. I wanted to knock the spatula out of his hand and make him bend me over something like he said he would.

I didn't know how to sit here and eat breakfast and drink coffee with that desire inside of me.

He was watching me, like he knew I wanted to run and he wasn't going to persuade me either way. Maybe he wanted to run, too.

"I've never made breakfast for another person," he said. And it was like his hand had snuck out of the shell he lived in and dropped a little breadcrumb onto the ground between us. And now I had to push my hand out of the shell I lived in and take the breadcrumb.

"Why don't I believe that?" I asked, and then winced. Shitty way to pick up the breadcrumb. "I mean...you host orgies. It only makes sense someone would get hungry. Or something."

"Not technically an orgy." He glanced down into his sizzling pan. "You need five for an orgy. Technically."

"Good to know."

"If you're going to leave, leave. But if you're staying I'd like a cup of coffee."

He addressed those words into his pan and I was glad, because I had to give myself a wicked eyeroll before stepping inside and shutting the door.

Honestly, after last night I was going to run scared? Grow up, Charlotte.

I poured coffee into the two mugs on the table. Each of them said Iowa State Wrestling on them. After I filled them, I took one over to Jesse.

"Did you go to Iowa State?" I asked, handing it to him so he could take the handle and not burn himself.

The look he shot over my shoulder was decidedly not smiley.

"Your mug," I said. "And you had a pair of shorts on once—"

He was wearing the same shorts now, I realized. The red Iowa State printed on the shorts right above his knee cap.

"Jesus, you pay attention to the details, don't you?"

"It's kind of my job."

He didn't say anything and I took a sip of coffee just so I had something to do.

"I went for most of a year," he said.

"What happened?"

"I got a scholarship so I went."

"No." So weird that he would frame my question that way, like the story was in how he went, not how he left. "Why did you leave?"

"Grades mostly. I pretty much fucked it up."

"What was the scholarship for?"

"Wrestling."

Oh, man. So many things clicked into place.

"All right. This shouldn't be too bad," he said and turned toward me with two plates piled high with food.

What he put down in front of me was such a surprise I could hardly believe it. Bacon, yes. Some potatoes but eggs, too, fried and covered in salsa and avocado. There were tortillas on a separate plate.

"Wow!" I said. "This is beautiful."

"Yeah?" He looked pleased as he sat down. "Beautiful might be a stretch. My mom used to make this for us on weekends. Hopefully it doesn't suck."

It totally didn't suck. And for a few minutes we were quiet as we ate.

"So is wrestling how you got into the fighting? In the basement?"

He kept eating, not answering for so long and I realized, this was just how he was. He didn't speak without thinking. He didn't answer questions casually. I put down my fork, compelled to pay attention.

"Yeah," he finally said. "I grew up around here. Wrestled in high school and when I came back from college, this old friend of my dad's, Sal...he reached out. Offered me the opportunity."

"Opportunity?" I sputtered and the second I did I knew it was a mistake.

He put down his fork. "I flunked out of college. Probably would have flunked out of high school if it wasn't for my brother. All I ever wanted to do was wrestle. It was all I was good at. So when I moved back here I could fight for Sal, or I could roll in with some gang, or I could work at McDonald's."

I swallowed the egg that was a lump in my throat.

"I'm sorry," I said.

"No," he sighed. "I'm sorry. I just...everyone thinks this thing I'm doing is a mistake. But it feels like the thing I'm supposed to be doing."

"Fighting?"

He rubbed at his forehead with the back of his hand. "Yeah. Fighting."

"You like it then?"

"I feel like my life makes sense when I'm fighting. Or training for a fight. Every other part of my life just feels like something I have to get through."

"I understand that," I said. "That's how I feel about my work too. Like it's the best part of me."

"Exactly."

"Do you...like, have a gym? Or something? A trainer? I mean, I don't know anything about what's happening in the basement but if I've learned anything from *Rocky*—"

"That's boxing."

"Yeah, I know, I'm just...if you're going to be serious about this, don't you need some guy in your corner to squirt water in your mouth? To tell you to do a few more push-ups? Hit the cow carcass one more time?"

He was smiling at me. "What?" I lifted a hand to my face, sure I had egg yolk on my chin.

"You talk a lot."

"I do." I winced.

"I like it."

Well, that was pretty nicely done.

"And no," he said. "I don't need any of that stuff. I'm all right on my own."

I looked up, about to argue because was anyone really all right on their own? Wasn't that the lie introverts told themselves? Being an introvert myself, I'd told myself that lie one or three hundred times.

"I felt that way before I got an agent. I had some work and I was making money, but when I got an agent it was like my whole life worked better because she was getting me better jobs and better pay. It's not exactly the same thing."

"It's not."

"But sort of?"

"No."

He was watching me so intently that I shrugged and went back to eating just so I had something to do. I noticed he did not go back to eating. And the vibe between us got chilly.

"You have a brother," I said, having polished off the avocado. There was never enough avocado if you asked me.

"Yeah. You got family?"

"Not here." I didn't want to talk about my sister. I wasn't supposed to be talking about my sister. I mean, it seemed so ridiculous that Jesse would have anything to do with the guy she was running away from, but I wasn't taking any chances. "Where's your brother?"

"Here. In the city."

"You close?"

"Not anymore."

"What happened?"

"I don't know, what usually happens? I disappointed him. He pissed me off. My parents aren't around to make us apologize. Who the fuck cares?" His words were hard and sharp. Little projectiles he threw at me.

"I'm sorry."

"Fuck, what are you apologizing for?" he snapped and I sat back. "Sorry," he muttered, dropping his fork on the plate. "I'm not good at this...shit."

"What shit? Talking to people?"

"Talking to people I want to fuck."

I blinked. Blinked again.

"Stop," he said with that laser intensity I'd grown to expect from him. Like he couldn't be bothered with peeling me apart and instead was just going to slice me right open. "Stop with the wide-eye act. Last night—"

"I don't do that kind of thing. On the regular."

"No shit," he laughed, but it wasn't joyful. Or kind, really.

"Why...why are you being mean?"

"Because I am fucking mean. What did you expect?"

"Okay," I said and stood up on shaky legs. "This was a mistake."

"Running away?" he asked. "How am I not surprised?"

"You're being awful. Am I supposed to just stay here and take it?"

He didn't say anything. Just sat back with his arms crossed over his gray tee shirt, and watched me. I stepped for the door and then remembered my bodum. I couldn't leave it here—it wouldn't survive in this hostile environment—so I reached back and grabbed it. Sloshing coffee on myself, but I barely felt it and could not care.

"Bye Jesse."

"Yep."

Numb, I got back to my apartment, unlocking and then shutting the door behind me when I was inside. I could be prickly when it came to talking about my family—but he was fucking nuclear. He just bombed that whole thing because he didn't want to answer questions about his brother.

I had issues, but jeez.

There was a knock at my door and before I could turn and answer it, it was open and Jesse was walking through. His face set like a man who had business to do.

And I was the business.

"What—?"

"I'm sorry."

"Okay."

"I'm not that guy," he said, stepping up to me, crowding me against my kitchen counter.

"What guy?"

"The fucking make breakfast for you guy."

"No kidding," I said with a smile like the slice of a knife. "What guy are you?"

But my body knew. My body knew what guy he was. And like he knew he didn't have to answer, he didn't bother. His mouth was on mine.

He kissed me like it was the end of the world. Like this was the last thing he was going to do on this earth before everything went up in smoke. And I'd never been kissed like that. And I'd had no idea what I'd been missing.

A kiss like this? Full-mouthed, lips and tongue and teeth, a hand gripped hard around my braid? This was something I could get addicted to. This was something I could stop my life in order to get. This...

This was sex. Sex the way it was in movies. And books.

I felt primal all of a sudden, and I realized that I was kissing him the way he was kissing me. My hands were fists in his shirt. I sucked on his tongue. Bit his lip. I ate him like he was an avocado and I was starving.

My back hit my fridge because he'd pushed me there. His

hand cupped my chin, lifting my head as he backed an inch away from my mouth.

"I'm sorry I'm a dick," he whispered, his breath washing my lips, my face. Covering me in his scent.

I swallowed back the words *I'm sorry I'm so sensitive* because I was tired of being that girl. The girl who made the people who hurt her feel better for having hurt her. I said instead, like I was in a movie: "Make it up to me."

His lip kicked up, his eyes got heavy. Dark. I could feel him against my belly. A hard thing and I pushed against him, just pressed my belly to his, trapping his cock between our bodies.

"Yeah," he said and licked my mouth. Not a kiss. A lick and I gasped, my skin on fire. My brain sparking and short-circuiting.

Jesse kissed my breasts, palmed them roughly in his rough hands. Bit the hard nipple through the silly fabric of my silly dress.

I gasped, a choked "Yes" coming out of my throat.

And then he was on his knees in front of me, pushing my skirt up. Hands cupping the backs of my thighs. Some sound gurgled out of my throat and I stopped breathing.

"Lift your skirt, Charlotte," he breathed and I did what he asked. With shaking hands I lifted my skirt until it was just his breath against the black silk of my underwear.

My eyes were closed, my head tipped back and when his tongue touched me, a tiny taste through the silk of my underwear, I jumped. I jumped and groaned, and he groaned and went back for more.

Guys had gone down on me before, sure. But they'd seemed sort of tepid events. Uncomfortable for everyone involved. Nothing like this. Not ever like this.

Not standing in my kitchen, with him on his knees in

front of me. Not through my underwear like some kind of electric barrier between his body and mine.

No one like Jesse.

"Spread your legs," he murmured and I did. And he licked me deep and hard, my underwear soaked. From him. From me. I twitched and moaned and he went back for more, his hands sliding up from my thighs to my ass, where he palmed me, gripped me.

Held me still.

And ravaged me.

I held my skirt with one hand and braced myself against the counter with the other. He pushed my underwear down to my knees and I had to swallow back cries as he found my clit with his tongue and slipped his fingers inside me.

I was made of lightning and fire. I was twitching out of my skin. The pressure inside my body too much to bear and I had to crack, something had to crack—and then he sucked me into his mouth and I came. I came so hard my knees buckled and I would have fallen if he hadn't caught me. His hands braced against my stomach.

Condoms, I thought. I didn't have any. And we were going to need some. A bunch. He stood up in one fluid movement, his hands leaving my hips to hold on to the counter behind me.

I was panting like I'd run up and down a flight of steps and he was staring down at me, his face...shiny. I stepped out of my underwear, leaving it a silk puddle on the floor.

"We need condoms," I said, watching his tongue part his lips to lick at what was left of me all over his face.

He shook his head and kissed me. Sweet and soft. "I'm sorry I was an ass," he said and stepped away.

"No, don't...leave. Not like that." I gestured weakly to the erection in his pants. I thought of the day when he'd fixed all my stuff and I'd had that little fantasy of going to my knees in front of him and I stepped forward, ready to give him that.

Wanting to give him that.

But he caught me. Shook his head.

"You don't want...that?"

His mouth quirked and he shook his head. "I was an ass to you today. That shit you said about your agent and me getting a trainer, you were right."

Oh God, my God that was so... gentlemanly.

"You shouldn't be scared of wanting more," I said. "Of thinking you deserve more."

"Well," he said, looking dubious, "let's not get carried away."

"You're forgiven and I want to give you something," I said. "Last night...today?"

He nodded, his face red and tight like he was just barely holding on, and I had no idea what was holding him back, but it was real. And he wasn't going to try and break free. His fingers on my shoulders slipped underneath the straps of my dress and slowly pulled them down, until they were limp against my arms.

"You can give me this," he whispered.

"What?"

"You can let me see you. Your body."

He found the zipper at the back and slowly, while I breathed hard in my throat, he lowered it. The bodice of my silly dress fell away and instinctively I caught it.

"No," he breathed, his eyes past dilated. He wanted to see me. Like this. In the milky sunlight coming in through my bumblebee curtains.

I let go of the dress and it fell down, away from my breasts. I caught it at my waist and wished that my hair was down instead of back in this braid so I could tilt my head forward and hide.

"Jesus," he breathed and lifted a trembling hand toward my breasts. They were big. And I never thought much of them. But Jesse seemed... transfixed. His fingers stroked the pale skin, a blue vein just visible under the surface. My pink nipples were hard and painful and he ran the backs of his fingers across one and then the other.

"I was right," he whispered. "You're so fucking soft."

"It's...they're..." I made some gurgling sound of despair and tilted my face away.

"Fucking perfect," he said. "Fuck. Charlotte. I'm sorry."

And then, like he couldn't stop himself he reached into his shorts, pulling the elastic band down so his cock sprang free and I stared openmouthed as he palmed his cock, stroked himself, hard and fast three... four times and then groaned.

His hand gripped my shoulder hard enough I might be bruised tomorrow.

And he came in gasping, grunting spurts. A white arc of come splashing against my dress. Against the bare skin of my stomach. Over his hand.

Immediately, like it was an instinct and nothing else I wanted to lick his hands, I wanted to taste his come.

"Fuck," he breathed, his head pressed down on mine and I could feel his sweat. "Sorry."

"No," I said, fast and eager. "Don't... don't be sorry. That..." I couldn't not grin at him. "That was really hot."

He laughed wearily and tucked himself back under his shorts. I began to shrug into my dress but he stopped me. He reached back behind his head and pulled his shirt off, in what had to be the sexiest way to take off a shirt ever in the history of both shirts and men, and then cleaned off my stomach. Wiping away what he'd left behind.

And then he did the same with his hands. Balling the shirt up in one hand when it was done.

"You all right?" he asked.

"Fine," I laughed. "Great."

"Someday," he said, "you're going to tell me what you're doing here."

"I told you... my boyfriend kicked me out."

"Why don't I believe you?"

Because I'm a shitty liar.

I blinked up at him, stunned a little that that was what he was thinking about and then, before I could formulate some lie, he was gone.

And frankly, I didn't know what I was doing here.

CHAPTER ELEVEN

Charlotte

It was a completely stupid idea. I totally understood that. Like in the pantheon of bad ideas, this wasn't like... nuclear bombs, but it wasn't quite as harmless as the Slanket either.

I'd had my hand smacked by Jesse plenty, I didn't need to go searching out more reasons for him to be a dick to me. Perhaps any other woman would think Jesse had some kind of personality disorder, and frankly I had plenty of evidence pointing me in that direction. But there was something about him, something in the way he watched me out of the corner of his eye that reminded me a little of... me.

And because I was an idiot, I put the curtains I'd picked up at the hardware store—that had been on super discount because they were dark and ugly as hell—and propped them against the door.

I was just going to leave them there, but then I realized if I did there was a 100% chance of them being stolen. Maybe

I'd knock and then run away, so when he opened the door they'd just be there.

Which was also dumb, because he'd know they were from me. Like some random stranger would go around leaving curtains against his door?

"This is so stupid."

"What is so stupid?" a voice asked over my shoulder, and I turned to find Jesse standing there. Dressed head to toe in gray sweats, drenched in sweat.

"You're not supposed to be running," I said.

His eyebrows lifted. "I'm not?"

Oh man. It was like I'd just confessed to stalking. "You just usually don't... you know...run at this time."

"I don't?"

Oh, okay. Now he was laughing at me and I felt the awful blush creep up my face.

"I'm not stalking you."

"Clearly."

"It's just our walls are thin."

He nodded. "They are."

"Stop laughing at me."

"Okay." He leaned forward and kissed me, a light brush across my cheek. Agreeable Jesse was more potent than angry Jesse, it was like having a furious dragon curl up in my hand. "I'm running more because I have another fight in two weeks."

"Oh." That news sent dread spinning through my stomach as I remembered his swollen busted-up hands from his last fight. The way he stumbled down the hall, his shoulder against the wall so he wouldn't fall over.

Awful. All of it awful.

"That explains what I'm doing outside my door," he said. "What are you doing?"

"I bought you curtains," I blurted. "Stupid right? Just... make fun of me and I'll be on my way."

He pulled the ear bud out of his other ear and pushed the gray hood off his face and I had to look away. That's how handsome he was. How perfect and raw and hot.

My mouth literally watered.

"You bought me curtains?"

"Sure did. I mean, don't get excited, they were on super discount. I think they're... denim. Yep. I bought you denim curtains for like ten bucks."

He looked at me with this weird little smile on his face. "No one has ever bought me curtains before."

"Well, that's swell, I've never bought anyone curtains. But I just figure with the non-orgy orgies you have, you should have some nice thick curtains over your windows so weirdos like me don't just show up and watch..."

Oh. Shut. Up. Charlotte.

"You just can't stop talking, can you?"

"Nope. Not even a little."

He picked up the plastic bag with the curtains in it. The clearance sticker told him exactly how little I paid.

"It was stupid," I whispered, reaching out for them. I didn't know what to do with him. Where exactly he was supposed to sit in my life. Where I was supposed to sit in his. All I knew was that I wanted more of him. I wanted more sex. And more kissing. I wanted to stroke his hair and talk about wrestling and what made him so upset about his brother that he couldn't talk about him.

I wanted more of Jesse. More than I'd ever wanted from anyone else outside of my sister. I hadn't realized how much room Abby took up until she was gone.

"I'll take them back."

"Nope," he said and opened his door. He walked through,

leaving me behind him in the hallway, unsure of what was happening. "You can come help me put them up."

"I don't... there's no curtain rod."

"I've got duct tape," he said with a grin that was really the end of me.

I felt a little bit like I was making friends with a bear. Some creature that might snap my head off one minute or curl up in my lap the next, and I couldn't blame the bear for being a bear. Not really.

I could blame myself, because it wasn't smart to befriend a bear. I knew that. Perhaps it was simpler to have sex with the bear and avoid anything else. But somehow I bought the curtains. And somehow I walked right into his apartment.

In the bedroom, my breath hitched and my palms got sweaty and I fumbled with the package as I tried to open it. Jesse pulled the duct tape off the sheets on the wall, and the "curtains" fell to the floor, revealing Jesse's view.

The parking garage.

He stood staring at it for a moment, long enough that I noticed.

"You okay?"

He nodded and bent over, wadding up the sheets.

"You... nervous about the fight?"

"The guy I'm fighting... he's pretty legit."

"And you aren't?"

He grinned at me, letting me know how legit he was. "He's just got sponsors and shit, you know? A guy in the corner who squirts water in his mouth."

He tossed my words back at me with a smile that did nothing to hide how strangely uneasy he was. Pensive.

"Do you want that?"

He shook his head. "Never have before."

Which seemed to indicate now he did.

"I'm sorry for what I said yesterday. It's none of my business..."

He didn't say anything, so I let the sentence just fade into quiet.

"It's nice," he said.

"What is?"

"Someone giving a shit. About me."

"Well, let's not get carried away," I joked, but my eyes caught his and for a moment, I couldn't breathe. I couldn't feel my feet on the floor or the clothes on my body. That was the power of eye contact with Jesse.

"I don't talk about my family," he said. "I haven't for a really long time."

"I understand. I don't talk about mine, either. It hurts."

He faced me fully. "You haven't told me anything about them," he said. "Do you have a sister? Brother?"

"Can we...not?" I said. "I'm kind of... happy for the first time in a long time and I don't want to talk about my family."

He opened his mouth as if to argue with me, but then shut it and shook his head.

"Sure," he finally said. "Hand me the curtains."

I shook the denim curtains out of the plastic bag and handed him the edge with the hooks for the curtain rod. He ignored the hooks and tore a strip of duct tape off his industrial-sized roll and slapped it onto the wall.

As the curtains shook out, something seemed...wrong.

We got the other curtain up, the room getting dark as the denim did its job and kept out peeping eyes and most of the sunlight. As the curtains settled against the window I stepped back with a gasp.

"I'm sorry," I breathed.

"What the fuck is that?" We were both staring at the thing on the curtain.

"It's a...Minion. From the kids' movie."

A round-headed one-eyed Minion with a protective goggle.

Jesse tilted his head. "Kids like that thing?"

"I think so."

It was quite possibly the worst curtain for an orgy room that I could have picked out.

"Your face," he said with a laugh.

"This...oh, my god, let's take them down."

"Why? They make it nice and dark in here. I like it."

"You can't be serious."

"I'm pretty much only serious." He glanced back at the curtains—they were the actual living definition of ludicrous. "They're staying."

He turned and I shrugged. "It's your orgy room. You want a one-eyed cartoon character watching you, I guess that's your freaky business."

"I told you," he said. "Not an orgy."

"Potato tomato," I said, a little joke from my mom. He reached up and touched a curl that was brushing my shoulder, a white-blonde corkscrew. His pinky brushed my shoulder and he dropped the curl to tug down the tee shirt I was wearing. He tugged until he could see the mark he left on me. And I let him.

"I like that on you," he said.

"Me too," I told him.

"Yeah?"

I nodded, pretty speechless.

"I want to put more of these on you. All over you."

Sure, I thought. Let's do that.

Sun split through the space between the dark curtains, slicing right through his mouth as he smiled. I wanted to kiss him so badly I hurt.

"I've been thinking about yesterday."

"Me too," I breathed. He was tracing the edges of the

mark he put on me. Over and over again until it was practically hypnotic. I was completely under his spell.

"I'm gonna need to come on your tits."

I sucked in air like I was drowning.

"You gonna let me do that?" he asked.

"I'm gonna let you do everything," I whispered.

He groaned low in his throat like I was killing him, like I'd twisted the knife. Like I was simply too much.

"I just went for a run," he said, his fingers dropping from my shoulder. "I need to shower."

"Yeah," I whispered. "Sure."

He pulled the sweatshirt over his head, taking his shirt off with it, and his chest was damp and flush and right there. Close enough to touch. So I did. I touched the rounded edge of his pec, trailed my fingers over the ridges of his abs. Spread my hand as wide as it could go, my pinky in his belly button, the tip of my longest finger brushing his nipple.

I wanted to map him. Use my hands to discover the length and width of his bones and muscles. The curves of his spine, the arch of his foot. And my body, my skin, the far edges of myself ached to have him do the same to me.

I didn't get touched a whole lot in my life, and I was hungry for it. Dying for it.

He grabbed the hem of my shirt and started to pull it off. I put my hand on my stomach, keeping it down.

"You're taking a shower," I reminded him.

"You're coming with me."

I shook my head. If his shower was anything like mine, it was tiny and the lighting was like a department store change room. It was, without a doubt, the least sexy place in the Bay Area. I would not be going.

"I'll wait." Right here in this nice dark room. Perhaps under the covers even.

"I don't want you to wait. I want you to scrub my back."

"It's not...that...you can..."

He stepped back. Kicked off his shoes and in one motion pushed down his pants until he was standing naked in front of me, his cock twitching against his thigh. As I watched it grew erect, and I could have clapped like he'd performed a magic trick. But I knew if I lifted my hands from my shirt he'd be all over me.

"What's going on?" he asked.

"Nothing. Shower. I'll be here—"

"In the dark. Under the covers."

"Exactly." I smiled at him, pleased he got it.

"Bullshit. Is this some body nonsense about your belly or the way your thighs touch?"

I blinked, stunned that he knew. That'd he'd guessed, but then the demons in my head jumped up to say *Well, of course he guessed, he's looked at your body. He knows you're fat.*

"I just...it's bright in there," I said and blew out a long breath. "It's nice and dark in here."

He pulled me to him so hard and so fast I hit his chest and the air got knocked out of me. He held me so tight I was like one of those women in a 1940's movie, bent over his arm, so off balance I had to hold onto his shoulders.

He was sweaty and warm and naked and it didn't matter. Forget the shower, I thought. Let's just get to the sex. I moaned into his mouth, opening myself up to his tongue and his teeth the punishing nature of his kiss. And all of it told me what was going to happen to my body in the next hour. The way I would be used and held and fucked and I wanted it. All of it.

He leaned back and suddenly my shirt was off.

"What—"

"Shhhh," he said and kissed me again. My bra was gone, my skirt pushed down past my hips, my underwear with it. "I want to fuck this body," he said against my lips. "I am fucking crazy about this body."

He squeezed my ass as if to emphasize that point and I gasped again, and then—because really why was I arguing? Why did I care if he didn't?—I moaned my capitulation.

"That's right," he said. His dick so hard against my now-bare stomach. And he didn't so much lead me as half carry, half shove me toward his bathroom. And every second of his Neanderthal tactics wound me up, got me hotter. And like he knew, like he could taste it in my mouth or see it in my face—he only gave me more.

"Stand there." He turned me so I faced the mirror. He even went so far as to put my hands against the cold white porcelain of the old sink. "Don't move."

In the mirror I watched him flip aside the shower curtain and crank on the faucet. He held his hand out into the water, checking the temperature and adjusting. And then he turned toward me, and his eyes met mine in the mirror before they dropped to scan my body. I closed my eyes, imagining what he saw and kind of hating it.

"I didn't say you could do that," he whispered just before his hands came around me, cupping my breasts in his big palms. I moaned at his touch. "Open your eyes."

I was powerless to resist.

He stood behind me, his face buried in my hair, his hands so dark against the skin of my chest. "Look at how beautiful you are," he whispered.

I flinched away from him. "Don't."

He glared at me in the mirror. "No talking. No closing your eyes. You're not leaving. Watch."

The mirror was small so I could only see our faces, shoulders and the tops of my breasts, gripped in his dark hands. I couldn't see his hand slipping down over my belly. I moaned, my eyes slipping shut.

"Eyes open," he whispered, but I didn't do it right away and he stepped away from me, the searing heat of his body all along my back replaced by a cool breeze.

"No," I gasped, my eyes opening.

"You gonna do what I say?"

"Yes."

"Good. Watch. Keep your mouth shut."

So I did as his stomach pressed up to my back, his thighs against my thighs. His hand palming my belly, touching all the places I hated, and I could feel myself retreating, back deeper inside my body.

"Stay with me," he whispered, and that hand tormenting my belly slipped down between my legs. I gasped, arching back into him as his palm covered my pussy. I pressed my ass against his dick and ran wet when he groaned.

He fingered me, long and slow, circling my clit, slipping inside my body. My clit was buzzing, my body aching. I got up on my tiptoes, not sure if I wanted more or to get away. And the whole time I watched him.

And he watched me.

This dark specter over my shoulder.

Perhaps it was the mirror. That this all seemed to happen there, one-square removed from who we were. I don't know, but I didn't flinch and I didn't look away. I was nailed by his fingers deep inside me and his eyes, hard on mine.

"I'm gonna make you come," he whispered, licking the lobe of my ear, sucking it into his mouth. My knees buckled and his hands kept me upright. "And you come so pretty for me," he said. "Watch."

"I am."

"Not me. You."

A tiny shift. A small movement of focus and suddenly I was staring into my own blue eyes.

And the woman looking back at me was no one I had ever seen before.

Locked and torn and impaled and tortured.

Excited and sexy and confident and here. *Right here*. Not half in my head. Not in some fantasy workplace that was so safe and distant.

Here.

I smiled. Wide. Eyes dilated, blown out with lust.

I was here. And I wasn't going anywhere.

CHAPTER TWELVE

Charlotte

"Yeah," he whispered in my ear, pressing kisses along my neck, down my shoulder.

He squeezed my clit and I shattered, all around him. All around myself. The tiled room echoed with my gasping, moaning cries, and before it was over, before my legs had any strength back he had me turned around and in the shower. The hot water falling over my head, into my face.

He kissed me through the water and I drank him in. I wrapped my arms around his neck and just drank in his kiss.

"We got about ten minutes of hot water," he said and I smiled against his mouth.

"Work fast," I whispered, my hands slipping down his sides, over his ribs and the thick ridge of muscle at his hips. And then to his cock.

His eyes were dark and shuttered and I wasn't sure what he was thinking, and I didn't care all that much. I was wild for him.

In this shocking moment of understanding—standing naked in a shower with a man who could tell me to do anything and I would do it—I completely got my sister. The hormone-fueled decisions. The things she would do for men who didn't deserve them. If she felt like this... if she wanted some guy the way I wanted Jesse... well, then it just made sense.

I'd do anything, right now. Anything he asked to keep feeling this way.

To keep feeling this good. Powerful. Desired.

Connected.

I stroked him, slowly. The water making a slippery lubricant and he reached over my shoulder and grabbed a bar of soap, running it through his hands until he was completely soapy.

Me, I thought. *Touch me with those slippery hands.*

But he didn't. He ran them over his face, his hair, down his body, over his hips and ass. His hands knocked mine away and he soaped up his cock and then shifted sideways and washed it all off.

"Suck my cock," he said.

"What?"

"Do it."

See? This was me going on my knees in a bathtub, water in my face, running into my mouth, and I did what he said. I fucking loved it.

"Yes," he breathed as I gripped him in my hands, licked him with my tongue. "More."

I took him inside my mouth and he groaned, his hand coming around my neck. He held me—not hard, but not... soft, either. My breath caught in my belly and I waited to see what he would do.

Make me, I thought. I remembered Amber and Matt, the way she took him all the way down into her throat. I thought of that surrender and that intimacy and I ached between my legs. I ached so hard and so fast, I whimpered around his cock.

And then, like he read my mind, he applied just the smallest bit of pressure against my neck, pushing me into him. And as long as I did it, as long as I took him deeper and deeper into my mouth, he let up on the pressure.

But the second I stopped, he did it again.

Not forcing me. No, God, no. Just...making me. The distinction was thin but it was real.

My hands dropped his cock and slid up his thighs to the hard edges of his ass, and I took him as deep as I could and I grabbed onto his ass the way that he grabbed mine.

Like I just couldn't get enough.

And I couldn't.

"Fuck," he breathed. "Charlotte. You're killing me."

I leaned back, gasping for air, coughing. The water running over my shoulders was turning cold and I flinched.

"Come on," he breathed. He turned off the water, helped me and grabbed me a maroon towel with a tear in the hem. It said Iowa Wrestling on it, in yellow embroidery.

He dried me. Every inch. Before getting his own towel.

"I want to have sex," I said. Standing there with his towel over my shoulder. Watching him dry his back, water dripping like diamonds on the edges of his very short hair.

"Yeah?" he asked, smiling at me. He pulled the towel from around my shoulders and dropped his own on the floor. "Bedroom," he said, slapping my ass for good measure.

He was right behind me. That now-familiar heat at my back, melting all of my inhibitions and protests. All my petty worries and cares.

Who gave a shit about anything when there was this... *feeling* to be had?

At the edge of the bed, I stopped, his hands running over

my body again, and I turned to face him. Slightly afraid of what I wanted. Of what it might mean.

"I...ah...I like it when you...boss me around," I said, trying to meet his eyes but failing.

"Yeah?"

I nodded and at his silence I finally managed the eye contact. He was grinning at me. "Are you laughing at me?" I asked, though I knew he wasn't. Whatever this new thing was between us, despite the way I wanted this sex to go—it was nice.

It was friendly.

And one hundred percent mutual.

"Nope," he said. "Sit down on the bed."

I did, the springs creaking.

Right in front of me he cupped himself. Stroked himself. Slowly. Once. Twice. Finally I moaned. And he took his other hand and cupped it around my head, not gently this time. The fine hairs at the back of my neck were pulled and the sting was so sweet.

He pulled me to him, not giving me a choice. Not like I wanted one... And he held his dick out for me and I licked the tip, opened my mouth and sucked him back deep into my mouth. As far as I could.

"More," he breathed.

I whimpered.

"Relax, baby," he whispered. "Relax. You're so fucking perfect right now. So fucking good."

The order and the praise, it worked some kind of magic over me and I relaxed, taking him deeper than I thought I could.

"Fuck. I wish you could see this," he whispered. Both hands cupping my head as he slowly eased out and then eased back in and all I could do was relax. Breathe. And listen to him. And something about all of this—something about the surrender of it... well, belief just came. "You're so beautiful."

He said it, so it must be true.

He told me over and over as he fucked into my face until finally I pulled back. My eyes watering, my throat hurting. He let me go, such was his surrender.

"Please," I groaned and I lay back in his bed, the rumpled sheets a heap under my back that I barely noticed. "Please, Jesse. I need you. I need you so bad."

Perhaps those were magic words for him. Or maybe it was the way my legs fell open. I had no way of knowing. But he opened his bedside table and pulled out a box of condoms. Awkwardly he tore one off the strip and let everything else fall to the ground.

I ran my hand over my pussy, so wet and so swollen I nearly came at my own touch, but he knocked my hands away. Pushed me by my ass up higher on the bed and then crawled over me, holding his cock right to the entrance of my body.

"Ready?"

"Please—"

He put his head against mine and I wrapped my fingers around his wrist where he was braced against the bed by my head.

"I'm gonna try and be careful, but fuck, Charlotte—"

Oh God, it was too much. Way too much. I grabbed his hand where he was holding himself and I lifted my lips until I felt him thick and hard, stretching the entrance of my body.

He was big. So big. But my body was ready and we were both nearly breaking apart, and at the first touch of my hot wet body against his cock he groaned and pushed hard into me.

I arched my back. My neck bowing off the bed. So much. Too much, maybe. It had after all been a long time. Such a long time...

"Shhhh," he was breathing in my ear. "Take it. Take me. You can. You can, baby."

And I did. I took him all the way into my body.

Every time he moved, I moved. Every time he exhaled, I inhaled. Nothing in my life had ever prepared me for sex with Jesse. Nothing could have prepared me for what was I feeling. The connection. And when I tried to retreat from it, protect myself from this unbearable intimacy, his big thick hand grabbed my jaw, clumsy and rough and so perfect I felt like I might evaporate right out of my skin.

"Here," he groaned, like sentences were beyond him. "Stay here. With me."

How could I not? How could I not just throw open the edges of my body? How could I not just let him in, not just to my body but into all of me? Into my head and my heart?

In the end it was easy. It was the simplest thing I'd ever done.

I just stared into his eyes and I came and I came and I came, and he slipped inside my skin and ribcage. He found a home somewhere impossible.

Lying there ecstatic and replete, boneless and infatuated, I stroked his back and his sides while he pounded into me and then growled as he came. Every muscle in his body so tense and beautiful I put my arms around him because I had to hold him... for a while anyway. And I'd thought that as much as I'd taken him into my body, maybe he'd taken me into his.

It was a nice fantasy. The kind of dream a woman like me would make up. Half real, half not real at all. That was my specialty, after all.

My infatuation tipped into something more and I lay in his bed, listening to him breathe, sure that he had to feel the same way.

———

Jesse

Charlotte was strong under all that soft skin. She was smart under all that soft hair. And making love to her had been... intense. She liked it with a hard edge that maybe shouldn't have been so surprising, but I still felt sucker-punched by her surrender. I felt... lucky. Lucky to be the guy she trusted like this. Lucky like I'd been given an unexpected gift.

I hadn't expected to feel so sweet afterwards. Like I'd smoked a joint in the sunlight.

Like I'd had the shit kicked out of me but won the match.

Victory and submission all at once.

My chest heaving, I rolled over onto my back and stared up at the ceiling. My damp cock flopped against my leg. I reached down and took care of the condom. Tying a knot in the end without looking.

"Old pro at this," she said.

"I'm a slut, what can I say?"

She smiled. I smiled. We were two goons smiling at each other.

"Thank you," she said. "That was..." She trailed off like she just didn't have the words for what had happened between us, which made sense. I didn't really either.

She was staring at the ceiling, grinning like a fool and I felt some pretty chest-beating pride that I'd fucked her like no one else had. And she didn't even know... she didn't know the half of the shit I wanted to do to her. She didn't even know, right now, how much she would like it.

But I knew, and it was a sudden fever in my blood.

"Great," I said, filling in her blank with a lame-ass word, but my brain was pretty broken too.

"Was it?" She turned her head to face me, her eyes darting to mine and then away. "For you?"

I rolled over onto my side, my fingers stroking her hair and immediately getting tangled in the curls. She tried to help me get untangled but I just grabbed a fistful of her hair, careful not to hurt her and turned her face back toward me.

"You were so good, Charlotte," I told her. "So fucking perfect. Just like I knew you would be."

She beamed at me and to my surprise leaned forward and kissed me on the mouth. "You weren't too shabby yourself."

At the touch of her mouth, her hair in my fist, I felt interest in another round building but she pulled away with a sigh. "I have to get some work done today."

"You sure about that?" I asked, slipping my hand down over her hip, rolling her toward me so I could get a good grip on that beautiful ass of hers.

She gasped at my touch, her eyes going wide and unfocused, and I liked it. I liked it so fucking much.

"Maybe...maybe not right now," she whispered.

I laughed and kissed her with my open mouth, showing her what I liked. The earthy beast inside my skin. And she met me with her own earthy beast.

"I've never..." she whispered as I kissed her neck. Her ear. The skin under her chin. She really was soft all over. "This isn't like me."

I leaned back. Looked deep into her startled and wary blue eyes.

"You looking for permission to fuck the way you like?" I asked. "It's yours."

"And taking a day off work and...all of it. All of this."

"You keep doing things that aren't like you. Have you stopped to think that maybe you're finally acting the way you really are?"

Her eyes opened wide as though what I said hit her in a soft spot.

"How'd you get so smart?" she whispered.

I shook my head. "I'm not smart." I rolled over on top of her, my body soaking in the feel of her soft silk skin like a man drinking water before heading off into the desert.

She wouldn't be here forever. It was painfully obvious she didn't belong at Shady Oaks, much less in my bed. But I was going to enjoy the fuck out of her while she was here.

"I just don't believe in bullshit," I whispered. "If you want something, take it. Do it. Have it. What does pretending you don't want something get you?"

"Keeps me safe," she whispered. "Keeps me from getting hurt. And I know you understand that."

I shook my head, denying it even as I knew it was true. She did too.

"The trainer?" she asked. "Sponsorships. You want that stuff."

I did. And I'd never let myself want that stuff before. Not until her. And with that thought I realized I had a ton of dreams and wishes hidden away, unsaid, barely thought about, in fear of the pain having them ripped out of my hands would bring me.

"What are you afraid of?" she asked, her hands rubbing through my hair, first one way and then another. Goose bumps rose up on my back and I closed my eyes because it felt so good to be petted like that. Her fingers traced my ear, the side of my jaw, and then wandered back up into my hair again.

"My brother." With my eyes closed, resting up against her body, it was easy to talk about.

"You're scared of him?"

"No, I mean, not really. Not that way. He's a bad guy, but he's not after me."

I'm afraid he might be after you.

What am I doing? I need to be getting her out of here, not keeping her in my bed.

"Sounds scary," she whispered.

"I'm scared that he's so far gone that way, I'll never get him back. That...it's over for us."

I'd never said this out loud. I'd barely even thought it in a sentence. It had just always been this thing in my stomach. This vague pain, sharp at times. Mostly dull. But always there.

But I said those words out loud and nothing happened. There was no lightning bolt or stone rolling toward me.

I just said the words and felt better for having said them.

She hummed and kept stroking me. So I turned my face into her neck, inhaled the smell of her—sweat and sex and something under that that was girly and sweet.

"I'm scared I'll get hurt in that basement and I'll never have a chance to be anything more."

"So stop," she whispered, her breath in my ear. I expected those words, they were the same words I would have said to her. The same words any sane person would say.

I opened my eyes, shaking off the power of her spell.

"I don't want to stop fighting. I just..." These were things I never said. Never even thought.

"I get it," she whispered. "You just want a little more for yourself."

That was it. Exactly.

"It hurts sometimes," she said, "trying to have more."

She parted her legs for me, her knees bending up against my sides. I kissed her neck. Bit her other shoulder. Sucked her skin until she moaned, until I felt the blood rise up against her skin.

"What's a little pain?" I asked, because this is where I lived—she lived there, too. I could see it in her face. Her eyes. The way she carried herself.

In the place between what we wanted and what we had.

And this is where all the pain lived.

Her blue eyes were wide and uncomprehending, so I spent the afternoon giving her a lesson in how a little pain could feel so fucking good.

CHAPTER THIRTEEN

Charlotte

I was twenty-five years old and I had just figured out how I liked to have sex.

I wasn't a virgin. I lost that in Matt Chapman's basement after a high school dance. I'd had a few boyfriends. I masturbated. I'd even, in college, kissed a girl. So, how...how in the world had I not known what I liked, what I wanted?

He'd put a finger in my ass and I'd seen stars. STARS! I'd come so much I pulled a muscle in my thigh. He'd moved me around like I was full of feathers.

He'd fucked me until I sobbed and he stroked my hair and told me how beautiful I was.

I was spending the day after being fucked silly trying to act normal. I answered emails. Did some edits on the pages. I called my parents.

But underneath everything was this constant hum of memory. Of my body on fire.

My body being sore. On the *inside*.

I stared at my mailbox, the cool October breeze lifting my hair and settling it down around my neck, and I remembered exactly what his hand felt like on the arch of my foot.

"Hey." Jesse's voice snapped me out of my daze and I actually jerked, that was how deep my daydream had gone. I turned away from my mailbox and found him behind me. My body shaking and warm and at the sight of him, wearing the hoodie and the sweatpants...ready.

Just like that.

I was sore. My body bruised and chafed and raw from yesterday and still I would have more if he let me.

I was an addict.

"Hey," I said with a forced awful laugh.

He grinned at me, his eyes knowing. "What are you thinking about, Charlotte?" he whispered.

Your hands. Your body.

Nothing, rose to my lips. The lie I would have told. But instead I caught myself and said, "You."

He leaned forward and kissed my shoulder. My neck. "Good," he said.

He opened his mailbox and took out some junk fliers. I did the same, reaching into my mailbox only to find an envelope from my agent.

The next part of my advance.

Five grand. Enough to get me out of this place. I could rent an apartment in my old neighborhood. Or at least in a neighborhood more like my old neighborhood.

This was how I got back to my old life.

The octopus and the coffee girl that didn't know my name. The fruit stand fantasy.

That had been my plan all along. Shady Oaks was temporary.

But what was I supposed to do when that old world wasn't nearly as satisfying as this one?

"Something good?" Jesse asked and I jerked my gaze away from the envelope toward him. My fantasy made real. My flesh-and-bone addiction.

I wasn't done with him. With this... with who I was becoming in this place.

"You're staring at that envelope like you can see through it," he said.

"Just... publishing stuff."

I could feel him watching me, as if waiting for me to tell him more. But I didn't. Because I shoved that check in my purse and picked up my grocery bags at my feet.

After the tremendous calorie burn that had been yesterday, I woke up this morning craving steak and chocolate cake. And now I had a bag full of those things, plus the stuff for a spinach salad and a baguette.

Because even in the bad neighborhoods in the Bay Area, you could get fresh bread.

"You having a party?" he asked.

"No. Just...dinner. I had a craving for steak and chocolate cake."

"Good craving."

"You want to come over?" I asked. Brave and bold, just like I was learning to be. "I have more than enough."

"You gonna cook dinner for me?" he asked, stepping up to me like he liked the idea. Like he wanted to cuddle up with the idea.

"Sure," I said. "You gonna make me come, if I do?"

He growled and laughed low in his throat and I could not believe this was me. And I could not be happier. Seriously, I was giddy as this person.

I kissed his smiling lips and decided I would hold onto that money a little bit longer.

This world...it suited me just fine right now.

———

Later that night, after we'd eaten dinner at his apartment and come back to mine to have sex, we lay in my bed, sheets pushed down to our feet. Sweat cooling on our bodies.

"You're so comfortable in your skin," I said, pulling the sheet up to cover myself.

He pulled the sheet out of my hands. "You should be too."

"I don't live like you do," I said. "In my body like that. I live in my head."

His soulful eyes took me in and then he nodded, like he could see that about me.

"Wrestling," he said, like that was the reason for his comfort.

"Illustrating," I said, like that was the reason for mine.

We both laughed and I took some comfort in knowing— or at least thinking—that he was laughing more with me than he had before. Just like I was laughing more with him.

"I want to see that picture," he said, rolling toward me.

"What picture?"

"The one of the *Where's Waldo* thing, but with the woman? In the park?"

"You want to see some of my work?" I asked. "Now?"

"Why not now?"

"I...I guess... sure," I said.

I got up off my bed and shrugged into the dress I'd been wearing before Jesse all but ripped it off me. He started to get up too, pulling on his underwear that I'd almost ripped off him.

He clearly intended to follow me to my desk, and I thought of that picture of my sister and me on my desktop.

What harm, I wondered, would it cause for him to know about Abby? It would be a relief to tell him. I hated this secret between us. Not that I wasn't sure he had his own, but this... she was my twin. The most important person in my life and the entire reason I ended up here, at Shady Oaks.

But I imagined telling him. I imagined somehow letting my sister into this thing that we had between us. I imagined telling him the stories of how we grew up. The jokes and the way I mothered her. Or really... what I imagined was letting myself, the version of myself I was when I was with my sister, into this thing with me and Jesse, and I shook my head.

Hating the idea.

I liked this version of myself. This not-drag me.

And if Abby was here, even in spirit, I didn't know if I could hold onto this new me.

"Stay here," I said. "I'll bring a printout."

He lay back down, arms behind his head, looking so perfect in my flowered sheets.

"Go," he said. "You sex fiend."

I smiled, delighted all over my body. In every square inch I was flush with happiness. With a kind of giddiness I'd never felt before.

I grabbed three of the printouts from my easel—Newgate Prison, Hyde Park, and the Palace. They were the three I was proudest of.

Back in the bedroom, I spread the three of them across the foot of the bed and Jesse, in that kind of animal way he had, shifted around so he was sitting in front of all three of them.

"Who am I looking for?" he asked.

"Her." I pointed at the Jane Austen in the palace. Her red bonnet, the book in her hand. The sort of knowing grin she wore, like all was according to plan.

Jesse grunted and looked over at the prison.

"Jesus," he breathed.

"Dark, huh?"

"Good." He looked up at me with wide eyes. "It's so

fucking good. It's creepy and it's cool." His fingers ran over the galleries and then he found Jane, near the area where the female prisoners could be outside for limited times each day.

He looked over at Hyde Park and found her almost immediately in the rowboat with the gentleman working the oars.

"Well, that was maybe too easy," I said.

"She looks like you."

"What?"

"Yeah. That grin of hers. It's like you."

"Stop," I laughed.

"I'm not joking." Carefully he stacked up the pages and set them down beside the bed and then he grabbed my hand, pulling me off balance, and then across his body as he sprawled backwards.

He pushed my hair off my face, holding it back in his hand like he did when I was giving him a blowjob. Just that tension, that sting made me pant.

"You going to tell me now?" he asked.

"Tell you what?"

"What you're doing here. What you're hiding."

I blinked at him, struggling to find the words to keep the lie going. But then all of a sudden, I put my head down in his neck. My nose right there at the spot under his ear.

"Not yet," I said.

"But you will." It wasn't a question and I nodded.

I would. Someday. When I was convinced that this version of myself would still be here when I was done.

———

Jesse

Ramirez was apparently tweeting shit about me. Amber was

big on letting me know what was happening on Twitter or Facebook.

"Seriously, dude," Amber said from where she was stretched out on my bed, scrolling through shit on her phone. "You can't let this stuff go without comment."

"Yeah," I said, dropping my towel and pulling on some underwear. I'd just finished working out and my body was loose and tired. "I can."

"You know," she said with a sigh, "if you went legit and had sponsors and shit—"

I turned to her, pulling up my sweatpants. "You're the third person to say that to me this month."

"Well, fuck man," she said. "You put Henderson down last month. You do the same thing with Ramirez, I think people are going to come knocking on your door."

"Ramirez isn't Henderson," I said.

"You scared?" she asked, her face twisted like the idea was ludicrous.

I left the room.

After yesterday all my fears were close to the surface. All my monsters rising from the deep where I kept them.

I didn't trust myself like this.

"We gonna fuck or not?" she asked, and I winced at how loud she was. Charlotte could have heard that. We'd spent most of the day yesterday in bed, wearing holes in her sheets and fucking each other so right I couldn't even imagine sex with Amber right now.

"Not," I said, looking into my fridge. It was just about empty. I grabbed a frozen burrito and put it in my microwave. A trainer would have me on a diet. Some kind of high-protein thing. Lots of vegetables.

The trainer would not appreciate my frozen burritos.

Amber came stomping out of my bedroom. "You are no fun anymore."

I grinned at my microwave. I was fun. Just not with her.

Charlotte and the way she gave me her body. The way she came for me like it was such a surprise every time... I could not get enough.

My loose, tired body was no longer quite so loose.

"See you around," I said to Amber as she grabbed her keys and purse.

"Yeah, see you in two weeks." She paused by the door and I turned toward her, surprised to see her seem to be biting her tongue.

"You got something to say?" I asked.

"I dig this shit," she said. "The fighting and the stuff after. But... Jesse, you're good. Really good. You shouldn't be scared of trying to get a little something better for yourself."

And then she was gone.

And my microwave dinged as I stared dumbly at the door.

I left the burrito uneaten in my microwave. Grabbed a stack of condoms in my bedroom and went over to Charlotte's place. And the thing I wasn't looking at, the thing I wasn't interested in, was why.

Because it was sex. Yes. Of course. I wanted to fuck her six ways to Sunday.

But there was something more.

There was something about the way that Amber said I should reach for something better and I immediately thought of Charlotte. And yeah, I knew Amber was talking about finding myself a club. Some sponsors. Real money and real fights. With rules to make sure my career in this brutal fucking business would last as long as I could make it.

But I was thinking of Charlotte.

About how fucking good and decent and real she was.

And I could not get enough of that.

So I left my apartment and knocked on her door. To fuck her.

To pretend for just a few minutes that Amber was right. That Charlotte was something I could have. Should have.

Despite knowing, deep in my gut, that these things we weren't talking about—they would end us.

Her door opened and Charlotte was there, looking... fucking delicious. Rumpled and messy. She had this knot between her eyes that gave her the impression of a stressed-out mouse.

I loved it.

She blinked at me.

"Jesse."

"Charlotte."

"What...what are you doing here?"

"I want to fuck you."

She laughed, a bright wild crack of sound that made me smile at her. Really smile.

"Oh, well in that case, come on in." She opened the door wide and stepped aside so I could come in. I felt like I always did when I walked into her place. Like I was walking into another world. Some kind of opposite dimension of my world.

"I need to finish a few things," she said. "Really. I mean... I'm not putting you off, but I have this..." She looked at her watch. "I have this deadline."

"Cool. You can work. I'll just...hang out."

We both realized how ridiculous that sounded even as I said it. Her place was soft and lovely and all the things my place wasn't. But she didn't have any fucking chairs.

"Go work," I said. "I'll be right back."

She nodded and scooted back over to her computer. She was wearing yoga pants and a flannel shirt that shouldn't look so hot on any woman, but on Charlotte, it looked delicious.

But then, I liked her in dresses with suns on them, so clearly I was fucked in the head.

Back in my apartment I grabbed one of the few things I'd kept from the old house. It had travelled with me to Iowa and back and now, more than often than not, it sat forgotten in the corner of my bedroom.

Dad's old bean bag chair.

It was made out of fake blue leather and duct tape, and I heaved it over my shoulder and took it back over to Charlotte's. I pushed open the door to her apartment, and her little head popped up between her monitors.

"I shouldn't be long," she said.

"It's cool, don't worry."

I locked the door behind me and tossed the bean bag chair in the corner of the room and sat—gingerly, very aware of all the tears under the duct tape—in it.

"Wow," she said. "I haven't seen one of those in years."

"I know," I said, wiggling my ass a little, finding a comfortable spot. I'd forgotten how comfortable this thing was. It had sat in our TV room for years. Mom hated it, Dad loved it.

Most of the tears in it were from Jack and I wrestling with it.

"Where'd you find it?" she asked.

"It was my dad's." Her head came up, like a puppy's smelling dinner.

"You don't talk about your parents."

I laughed. "Neither do you."

Truthfully, we didn't do a whole lot of talking when we were together. "Are your parents around?"

I shook my head. "Dead. Mom when I was a kid, Dad…a few years ago."

"I'm sorry."

I shrugged like it was no big deal, but the weight was heavy on my shoulders. "Where are yours?"

"Florida."

"Living the dream?"

"Something like that. I'm so sorry, Jesse. I need to get this done. They had a few edits for me," she said, looking at her screen but talking to me. From where I sat her face was illuminated by whatever was on her screen, and she looked paler than usual. "And the turn around was tight because they are sending out a few sample pieces to reviewers. A buzz thing, apparently."

"That sounds good," I said.

"It does, doesn't it?" Her voice had absolutely no enthusiasm in it.

"You're not excited?"

She glanced at me, her lip between her teeth. "You really want to talk about this?"

I blinked, surprised. Not so much by the question but that she had the stones to ask. "Yeah," I said. "I do."

Because I did.

I wanted to talk about whatever she wanted to talk about. I wanted to just sit here and drown in her soft little world.

"They want me to go on tour," she said.

"A book tour?" That sounded pretty fucking legit. I could just imagine Charlotte in her glasses, her hair all wild around her shoulders, talking to a room full of people about her weird amazing book.

"Yeah."

"And you don't want to go?"

She shot me a "give me a break" look. She didn't like people either. One of the many things I was completely surprised we had in common.

"They're just people."

"Hilarious, coming from you."

"This is a big deal. Seems a shame to be too scared to take it."

"I'm not scared."

"Bullshit."

She scowled at me and I shrugged. "Call it like I see it. You got any beer or anything?"

"There's a bottle of red wine on the fridge."

I wasn't much for wine but I stood up and got it anyway. "You mind?"

"No," she said, absorbed back in her screen. "Go right ahead."

"You want some?"

"Sure... maybe a little."

I opened the wine bottle and opened her cupboard, looking for a glass.

"You've got real fucking wine glasses," I said. I flicked my finger against the edge of one and it tinged.

"I do."

"You know what half the people here drink booze out of?"

"Coffee cups?"

"The bottle. And a brown bag."

"Are you mad because I have wine glasses?" she asked, and I realized how mean my voice was. "You don't have to use one. Drink out of the bottle. I don't care."

I poured us each a glass in her nice glasses.

"I'm not mad because you have wine glasses," I said. "I'm mad because there's shit you're not telling me."

She didn't meet my eyes—she pretended to be absorbed in whatever she was working on. I knew the difference between when she really worked and when she was pretending. This was total bullshit. But I didn't push, because I had plenty of stuff I wasn't talking about either.

"Here," I said, putting the glass down by her elbow. I took mine and sat back down in the bean bag chair.

My imaginary trainer who didn't like my burritos told me not to drink this wine.

One of the perks of not having one, I thought and drank from the glass.

The wine burned going down. But it sat in my stomach nice and warm.

"So?" I asked. "What are you scared of? With that book tour thing?"

She scowled at me. "I don't want to talk about this."

"I do."

"Well," she said, grinning at me, an evil little grin that got my blood pumping. "What if I wanted to talk about your brother?"

I laughed at her bravado. "Not gonna happen."

"Well, neither is talking about this book tour."

I took a sip of wine and she went back to her work.

"But you're going to do it, right?" I asked.

"No!" she cried. "No. I'm...not going to do it."

"But you want to."

"No, I can...see the merit in it. But I don't want to."

"Like you didn't want to watch Amber blow Matt?" She shook her head, her cheeks getting red. If I touched them, they'd be hot. "Like you do, but you're scared."

"No. Not like that at all."

"You're such a liar."

"What if no one comes?" she asked. "What if people laugh? What if I vomit all over the place? Or fall down? Or can't answer anyone's questions? What if—"

"Does that stuff happen on book tours?"

"It might happen on mine."

"Why do you get all the bad shit?" I asked. "Like, what makes you think that's what's going to happen to you? You've got this awesome career, doing this awesome thing and it's like you don't see it."

She looked back at her screen, mutinous and close-mouthed. "You're not going to get fucked this way," she said, all prudish. I wanted to laugh at her, because she'd melt under my hand and we both knew it.

"You have a fight coming up," she said.

"I do," I said, sensing a massive change in conversation.

"Do you... the thing with Amber and Matt... does that happen after every fight?"

I narrowed my eyes, wondering which way she was going with this. "Not every fight. Most."

"How...how did that start?"

"Amber's a medic. The guy that organizes the fights, Sal, he pays her to be there in case something bad happens. She likes to fuck fighters."

"And Matt?"

"Matt likes to fuck fighters, too."

"So... you're bi?"

I smiled at her, but felt my teeth on edge. I didn't peg her for this kind of person. "Are you bothered by that?"

"No!" She looked up at me wide-eyed. "No, I'm not bothered. It's consensual adult stuff. There's nothing for me to be bothered by."

That was a pretty good answer. "So what are you bothered by?"

"Are you going to do it after this fight?"

"It's not like we make a plan, it just kind of works out."

She hummed in her throat.

"Do you want it to happen?" I asked. "You interested in watching again?"

"I don't want to watch you fuck another woman," she said. "Or a man. I don't want you to do that at all... while we're... you know?"

"I know," I said.

"If we're together like this, I don't want you to be with anyone else. And I don't want to be with anyone else either. Is that... like a deal breaker for you?"

"You done working?" I asked.

"Just... a few more seconds." She tapped a few keys. A few more. She hit one key pretty hard and then sat back with a sigh. "Done."

"Come here," I said, motioning her over to me. And she came, spreading her legs to sit on my lap on the bean bag chair. She looped her arms around my neck and I pressed one quick kiss to her mouth.

"I'm not fucking anyone while I'm fucking you. And you..." I kissed her again, getting into it. "No dates. No dressing up in those jeans for other guys."

"I dress up in those jeans for me."

I hummed in my throat, liking the idea.

She sat back just as things were starting to get interesting.

"So," she said, tucking hair behind her ear. "Your fight is on Saturday, right?"

"Yeah."

"Can I come watch?" she asked.

"You want to?" I asked, dubious as fuck.

"Yes." She didn't hesitate or anything.

"It's pretty rough."

"I gathered."

"Is that...is that hot to you?" I asked. I mean, it was most of why Amber was sticking around me. She and Matt could go fuck anyone, but she liked shit rough and a little scary.

I was the rough and scary.

She was silent for so long that I realized it had been a dumb question. Of course that was why.

"Well," I said, wondering why I was so fucking angry by her non-answer answer. "You saw me after. I'm not in the best of shape for fucking. Not the way you like it." Though I'd given it my best shot, mostly in an effort to scare her away.

"I don't...that's not why I would like to go."

Like I was some wild dog waiting for a beat down, I watched her out of the corner of my eye.

"Amber dumped you on me afterwards, like..." Charlotte blew out a breath. "Like you didn't matter to her."

"Well, it's not like Amber cares," I laughed, the idea funny to me.

"I care," she said and my laughter dried up. "Maybe I'm not supposed to. Maybe that's not how this works, but... I care. And you're pretending you're not nervous, but...I can tell you are. You're nervous about something."

I spun the glass around in my hands, afraid in a way to look directly at her. Like she was the sun and my eyes would fry. Or she was something I wanted—really wanted—down deep where all the old things lived and breathed but I pretended that they didn't.

"If you don't want me there, I won't—"

"I want you there." The words erupted from my throat. My belly.

She put her arms around me, hugging me close. My hands went immediately to her hair, pulling out the heandband and the ponytail holder she liked to wear, until those crazy curls all fell down around her shoulders.

"I want you to go on that book tour," I said.

"Why do you care so much about the book tour?" she asked with a laugh that did nothing to disguise her worry. Her fear.

"Because I care," I said.

I kissed her and I took those clothes off of her and I spread her out on the floor like she was my personal feast and I kept us busy so we wouldn't say anything else.

Wouldn't confess any more of our feelings.

Wouldn't give away any more of our wounded hearts.

CHAPTER FOURTEEN

Charlotte

What, I wondered, does a woman wear to an underground fight club held in the bottom level of a parking garage?

I stood in front of my closet, wrapped in a towel, at a total loss.

The sunshine dress was out. The Big Bird tee shirt. The overalls.

In the end I grabbed what I'd worn on my last torture Saturday. The tight jeans, slinky top and the leather jacket. I wore my hair down because Jesse liked it that way.

My stomach was a ball of nerves, my hands were sweaty. I'd been imagining scenes out of *Fight Club* all day. I'd been trying to remember all my basic first aid, like that would matter. I'd been trying to imagine what people would think when we walked in together. And I'd been trying not to feel... excited about that. Proud of that.

Proud, in a weird way, of Jesse. Of being the girl he picked. Of having the guts to pick him.

I did my makeup with a heavier hand than usual, and the person looking back at me in the bathroom mirror was a sexy stranger with my eyes, and I dug that like crazy. I grabbed my boots and sat at my computer to put them on.

The picture of my sister and me on my home screen made my heart ache with a nearly impossible pain. A breathtaking grief. She would love this if she was here. She would love seeing me with someone, she would love seeing me happy.

Because I was. I was happy.

Part of me, insidious and small, wondered if I would be this happy if she was here. If I would have even taken the risk with Jesse. Or would my time have been tied up in Abby? I didn't like thinking that thought. It felt disloyal.

Still, my boots on, I turned my chair fully toward my screen and opened up the Facebook message that I'd never deleted.

My *I need you* message was still not responded to, and if it was in fact a spammer, they weren't trying very hard.

Feeling as if I'd settled down somewhere outside of myself, on the very far edges of the life I'd been telling myself all along that I liked while at the same time feeling almost wholly unsatisfied, I typed a message to Cheetara...

I think I'm falling in love. It's so weird. I know. I mean, we barely know anything about each other. I haven't told him about you, or what my life was like. He refuses to talk about his family. He's a fighter, can you believe that? Like a fighter in an illegal fight thing in the bottom level of a parking garage. I'm going tonight... I'm nervous for me. Scared for him. I don't know what I'm doing.

And the sex... oh my god, Abby. The sex.... I mean, if this was what you were chasing with all those boys I get it. I so get it.

Suddenly typing that made me wonder if my feelings for Jesse weren't really more about the sex than anything else. That made more sense than me falling in love with Jesse.

Never mind about the love thing, I typed. *I think I'm just drunk on sex. But in any case, I wish you were here to talk to. I'm sure you'd tell me to stop overthinking things, and I'm trying.*

I sighed and lifted my hands away from the keyboard and then, because I was on some kind of confession roll, I typed:

I really want him to like me the way I like him. Which is scary, you know. Because it seems so impossible. A guy like him and a girl like me...? I mean, how does that work?

"Enough," I said and pushed away from the desk. I wasn't going to go down into that basement in some kind of pity party.

I turned off my lights and locked the door behind me and knocked quietly on Jesse's door.

"Come in!" someone shouted and I entered Jesse's quiet and dark apartment. In the living room Jesse was sitting on the couch while another man sat on the coffee table, wrapping and taping Jesse's fists.

"I don't want to interrupt," I said.

"You're not," the man on the coffee table said. He glanced at me and did a quick double take. "Holy shit."

I blinked several times, stunned by his reaction. Jesse scowled at the guy. "That's Charlotte," he said, like he'd told this guy about me.

"Really?" the guy said and shook his head. "I'm sorry. I just thought you were someone else for a second. I'm David."

"Hey David," I said with a wave.

David nodded and went back to wrapping Jesse's hands, but every once in a while he glanced back at me.

In the dim room, my silver shirt sparkled and Jesse looked at me and smiled.

"That's for me this time."

I blushed at the ownership in his voice, and David glanced up at Jesse like he too was surprised to hear that kind of thing in Jesse's voice.

"Where you from, Charlotte?" David asked as he wove the tape around and around Jesse's right hand.

"Here."

"South San Francisco?"

"No. I grew up in Oakland."

"Family here?"

"What's with the interrogation?" Jesse asked David.

"Just talking."

"Talk about something else," Jesse said.

"Where are you from?" I asked David before he could ask me something else.

"Few blocks from here," David said. "Me and Jesse and his brother Jack all grew up here. I wrestled with Jesse and Jack," he said. "I was stuck in the year between them."

"Oh, I didn't know...Jack wrestled, too."

"Well, he sucked," Jesse said, glaring at David, like he was trying to shut him up with his eyes.

"You set the bar pretty high," David said with a laugh. "No one was as good as Jesse. Your brother had other talents."

"Yeah, and how's that working out for him?" Jesse snapped.

"Maybe," I said, stepping into the suddenly cold atmosphere between them. Normally I'd shrink away from this kind of atmosphere. Make some excuse to leave, but somehow in the last month of living in this weird place, finding myself in some kind of relationship with Jesse, I found another way to handle the uncomfortable things—which was to just meet them head on. "Maybe we shouldn't talk about this."

"Great idea," Jesse said.

David nodded, and then to my surprise he turned back to me, tearing the white tape off with his teeth. "What do you do, Charlotte?"

"Besides go to illegal fights with Jesse?"

David laughed, though it was hardly funny. I felt like I was getting trapped in something.

"Let's go," Jesse said as if he didn't want me to tell David the answer.

Whatever, I got it, old friends had crazy dynamics. Jesse got to his feet. He was wearing a pair of skin-tight athletic shorts and a hoodie sweatshirt over top.

"Let's get your face," David said and dipped his fingers into a giant jar of Vaseline sitting beside him. He wiped those fingers over Jesse's eyebrows and over his ears.

"You good?" David asked.

"Yeah," Jesse said. "Thanks."

"All right," David said, picking up his shit like he was leaving. "Go get that asshole. I don't like the shit he's been tweeting about you."

"You're leaving?" I asked, a little stunned.

"Yeah," David said. "Jesse doesn't like people watching him fight. Except... you, I guess."

That put me in a pretty particular spot and there was nothing to say about it. Jesse turned back toward his bedroom and David stepped up to me. His finger up, his face angry. At me.

"Listen to me, bitch, I don't know what the fuck your game is but you leave this kid out of it."

I could only gape at him. "I'm not...there's no game."

"Jack's an asshole, I'll give you that. But Jesse's a good kid and he doesn't deserve any of Jack's shit falling on him. Got it?"

"I'm not...I don't know Jack. I've never met his brother."

"Right," David said, like I was scum. Like I had the power to hurt his Jesse. "See ya," he yelled at Jesse. "Nice to meet you, Charlotte," he said loud enough that Jesse could hear me. And then he was gone.

"You ready?" Jesse asked, coming back into the room, this time with sweatpants over the tight shorts and wearing a pair of Adidas shower shoes.

What the hell was going on? I wondered. What exactly had I gotten myself into?

"Having second thoughts?" Jesse asked, like he had been expecting it. And I realized how alone he usually was in this thing. And how hard it must be to have me come. Taking that away from him now would hurt him. Like it would hurt anyone.

"I'm here," I said. "I'm coming with you."

I put my hand around his paper-taped hand and together we walked out of his apartment.

———

The crowd was around the pool again, the two girls drinking wine. The big beefy Irish guys—brothers, Jesse had said—sitting with them, flicking bottle caps into the empty pool.

"Go get 'em, Jesse!" one of the guys yelled. "I got big money on you!"

"Teach that asshole what happens when he runs his mouth!"

Jesse lifted his hand in a kind of salute that seemed to acknowledge and answer at the same time.

The women looked at me with wide, surprised eyes and I shrugged with as knowing a grin as I could muster, which also seemed to acknowledge and answer at the same time. And then we disappeared down into the basement.

It was as terrifying as I imagined, dark and damp. I only barely managed to swallow my scream as a rat or something ran over my shoe.

"Why do you come this way?" I asked as we walked through a big metal door into the bottom level of the parking garage. I could hear people now. Music. It was still dim but there were brighter lights up ahead.

We walked past the cement posts toward the action, which was centered around what looked like an old boxing ring. There were industrial work lights set up around it, creating the only light in the whole basement.

"I don't need to make a scene."

"Isn't that the point?" I asked. I'd watched boxing and grew up with WWF wrestling after school—I knew the entrance was part of the show.

"The point is winning. The rest of it is bullshit."

How entirely Jesse of him to say that.

People started to notice us as we came in, turning to watch us, stepping out of our way as Jesse and I made our way toward the ring. And it was scary, sure, but it was also thrilling. The air in the basement was laced with salt and sweat and blood and lust and it wasn't air I could live on, but it was exciting to taste it.

"How come last fight you had a guy keeping guard outside my door and now you're letting me come down here?"

"I'm here, aren't I?"

"You're going to be pretty busy, aren't you? To worry about me."

"I could be half dead and I'd worry about you."

That—well, that was something coming from Jesse.

"And you, babe, you're tougher than I ever dreamt. There's nothing down here you can't handle."

I grinned, beamed really. Because it was true. I was tougher than I ever gave myself credit for.

An old guy met us at the corner of the ring.

"About fucking time," he muttered. He had a ring of white curly hair around a shiny bald head and he wore an old rain coat like he was Matlock.

"I'm not late," Jesse said.

The guy swore under his breath and Jesse asked a few questions about security and the profits at the door. He didn't ask about the other fights or the guy he was there to fight.

"We kicked out a few guys," the old guy said. "Too drunk."

Jesse nodded like that was good.

"Who's the girl?" the guy asked.

"None of your fucking business, Sal. Where's Hernandez?"

The guy pointed across the sea of white lights to the shadows on the other side of the ring. Another man, surrounded by a lot of people, jerked his chin up at Jesse and Jesse nodded back.

"Don't move from this spot," Jesse said to me. "Seriously, stay right here."

I nodded and then Jesse was gone, up onto the ring, through the ropes to the center where Hernandez met him.

"Where's the referee?" I asked, looking around for some official-looking guy to give everyone some rules.

Sal looked me over head to foot and said, "Where'd Jesse find you?"

I didn't answer and his lip kicked up in what might have been a snarl. "There are no referees," he said. "The only rule is fight until someone goes unconscious or until someone surrenders."

"You're kidding."

"Look where you are, sweetheart."

Right. Illegal fighting ring in the bottom level of a parking garage. Rules were not appreciated down here. I suddenly understood what Jesse said to me the other day in a whole new way—he was scared he'd get hurt because there were no rules. Nothing to protect him but himself.

And he wanted more. He was tired of being the only thing between himself and harm.

This understanding broke me open.

I spread my feet a little bit wider and rooted myself down

to the ground. I would stand here. I would sparkle in these shadows as proof, if he wanted, that he deserved more.

Jesse came back a few minutes later and started to strip. The music quieted down and so did the crowd, everyone gathering closer to the edge of the lights, not quite stepping into them as if everyone had an agreement about the dark being better.

He left his sweatshirt and sweat pants in a heap at my feet. Kicked off his shoes and was about to turn back to the ring when I put my hand against his stomach. Just a touch. I didn't mean to distract him or ask for anything. But he turned back to me, grabbed my head in his taped hands and kissed me like a man going off to war. He kissed me with his teeth and his violence and the flavor of fear roaring through his mouth.

And then he was gone. Up on the mat.

It took everything I had to keep my eyes open. To witness every brutal punch and vicious kick. The guy Jesse was fighting wore the same kind of shorts Jesse did, but across his butt he had the name of a supplement company. The same name was on a banner draped across the ropes on his side of the ring.

There was a guy standing there too. Yelling advice.

A coach.

Jesse had me in the shadows holding his clothes.

The other guy landed something awful across Jesse's face, and he stumbled back and then back again as the guy punched him once more.

"Jesse!" I shrieked, my voice lost in the void. I held his sweatshirt up to my face, unable to watch, but then I pulled it down because that was the whole point of being here.

Jesse was backed into the corner, his hands covering his face, his body curled over itself as he did his best to protect himself against the vicious blows being rained down on him.

Jesse pushed off the ropes and the guy got him in some kind of hold, swept his feet out from under his, and Jesse went down onto the mat.

"Jesse!" I screamed again. Other people were yelling other things that made no sense to me, so I just screamed. "Fight him! Jesse! Fight him! Don't give up! Don't stop! You can do it, Jesse! You can do it!"

I had no idea what happened. No clue. Jesse was on the ground, the other guy on top of him. And then suddenly, Jesse had him flipped over on his back, his arm held in such a way that if the guy moved or Jesse moved it would break.

The crowd around me was completely silent. Still.

The guy pounded the mat and Jesse let him go.

The crowd went absolutely ape shit!

Glancing around at the wild-eyed faces around me, I missed Jesse getting up off the mat and through the ropes to me.

"Oh my god!" I cried when he was suddenly right in front of me. I didn't know if I should hug him or kiss him or what. He was bleeding, and I didn't want to hurt him any more than he'd been hurt.

He kissed me. He kissed me so hard I was imprinted with him.

And then he took me by the hand and led me away from the ring through the shadows toward our apartments. I raced to keep up. He was barefoot and half-naked and I was wearing high-heeled booties, carrying his clothes, and still we ran. We ran until we got up the stairs, through the basement door. He unlocked his door and pulled me into his apartment.

"Jesse!" I cried. "Aren't you supposed to stick around?"

He was stripping my jacket off me, and then my shirt.

"Don't you have to talk to people?" I gasped as he cupped my breasts in his hands, bent his head to kiss me there, where the mounds of flesh were pushed up against each other.

"No," he said, sweating and bleeding on me and I didn't care. I didn't care at all. "I heard you," he whispered, glancing up into my eyes. "I heard you yelling."

He was solemn and serious and I didn't know what it meant. But it meant something that I'd been there and I'd yelled. And he'd heard me.

"Of course," I whispered and I opened my arms to him.

He fell against me.

And I fell against him.

With Jesse I lived in a hundred percent of my body. Just like him. I felt him in every inch of my skin. I felt him inside my skin. He was in my skin and bones.

He pushed my leather coat off with his hands that were still taped, and the tape scraped the skin of my upper arms.

"Sorry," he breathed, panting and wild. He lifted his hands to his teeth and pulled at the edge of the tape, twisting his hand to unwrap it, and I stopped him.

"Let me," I said, grabbing the end of the tape and unwrapping his hands. Pulling it away from his skin. I did the same to the other hand, my head bent to see what I was doing, but of course—of course—I could feel him watching. I felt him standing there, panting, all his wild fierce desire barely restrained while I untaped his hands.

Once the last bit of tape was gone, he reached for me and I stepped back.

"Wait."

"Fuck. No—"

I lifted the sparkly shirt off my body, revealing the black lace bra that I thought was pretty fucking sexy and he groaned hard, which I took as agreement.

I unzipped my little booties and undid my pants, starting to push them off my hips.

"Wait," he said and he turned me, with his hands he turned me and then walked me over to the couch. "Here."

My back to him, I pushed down my pants, bending over slightly, giving the kind of show I never in my life would have thought I'd give. His hand cupped me, I felt his fingers against the skin of my hip, the heat of his palm against the lace of my underwear.

"Take these off too," he said, in a bossy mood tonight.

So I did.

"Bend over."

Oh, fuck. My belly trembled, my pussy was wet. The old insecurities wanted to plead their case, but I blocked them out and bent over, bracing my hands against the couch. I knew what was coming next, thought I was prepared for it, but when his palm hit the skin of my ass I shrieked.

"Shhhh," he said, stepping up closer to me, his body cradling mine. Heat and comfort. "I can't...I need you so much, Charlotte."

"Please," I whispered, looking back at him over my shoulder. I needed him too. Wanted him more than I ever thought I could want another person. He'd changed all my settings, turned everything up inside of me. "Fuck me. I need you to fuck me."

He fumbled with the condom, my slutty lover, undone with need for me, and my knees nearly crumbled with need for him. But then he was there, behind me, his hands at my hips, his cock at the entrance to my body and slowly, so slowly, he pushed inside of me.

And it was uncomfortable, it hurt even, because he was big and I wasn't totally ready. I stood up on my tiptoes looking for relief and it came when he put his fingers between my legs.

His thumb brushed my clit and I bit back a groan.

He didn't thrust inside me—he was still, his cock impaling me as I stood on my tiptoes. One hand between my legs, his other hand came up to my throat.

I was owned like this. Totally owned by him.

"Come," he said, his thumb riding my clit, pressing it into my body the way the two of us found out I liked. I groaned again and I knew he could feel it in his hand, the one around my neck, and I fucking loved it. I loved all of it.

"Yes," I gasped and I worked myself against him, fucking him when he wouldn't fuck me. The pain vanished and my body hummed and I wanted more. I wanted everything.

And like he knew—and fuck, he probably did—he let go of my throat and my clit and he grabbed onto my hips and he wrecked me. He pounded into me so hard the couch I was holding on to moved across the floor.

I screamed, over and over again and he didn't stop. I wanted to touch my clit so I could come but I couldn't let go of the couch in fear I would fall over. The tension inside of me coiled higher and hotter and sweat ran off my body and my throat was dry and raspy from my cries.

I had no clue what I was saying, but I knew I was begging him. I was begging him with everything in me.

"Fuck, come here," he said and he wrapped his arms around me and together we pivoted and he put us down on the bed. I was on my stomach, he laid down against my back, still inside of me.

Finally, I put my hands between my legs, touching my clit the way I liked, the way I needed, and within seconds I exploded, grinding myself between him and the mattress, squeezing him until he pushed down into me, fucking me as hard as I was fucking him.

"Jesus, God, yes!" he cried out, his mouth open against my shoulder. "Fuck. Charlotte. Oh, fuck, you're so good, baby. You fuck me so good."

I wasn't just replete, I was ruined. I couldn't move and didn't want to. Ever.

Something had changed between us tonight.

And it was everything.

———

The next day after the fight, we were both a little awkward around each other, not making a whole lot of eye contact, like we'd gotten drunk last night and revealed too much, but each of us wasn't sure what we'd revealed.

But it wasn't enough to make me leave him, and he must have felt the same way because he sure as hell wasn't letting me leave.

We moved to the couch in the afternoon to watch a movie. Jesse wasn't as beaten up as he'd been the last time, but he was moving real slow. And I was taking care of him like it was my job. Like it was the only thing I wanted to do.

And a little bit—it was. A lot it was. I wanted to lock the doors and watch shitty movies, order Chinese food and put ointment on his scrapes.

"You don't have to do this for me," he said as I rubbed more cream into the scrapes along his chin and forehead.

"I like doing it," I said. "Unless...you want me to stop?"

"No! I just...no one's ever done this."

No one had ever taken care of him, and that's why he didn't know how to take care of himself. Just like no one ever expected more from me, so I never expected more.

I kissed his lips and we curled up on the couch and we held the world at bay for as long as we could.

But there was a life outside the door and it was calling.

"I just need to check some emails," I said, when the first of the *Fast and The Furious* movies ended. I glanced down at his face when he didn't answer and realized he'd fallen asleep with his head in my lap. I stroked his head for a moment, the rough bristle of his hair. The hard curve of his skull.

When Abby and I were teenagers, she'd always had a

boyfriend on the couch with her in the back TV room of our house. Some football player or marching band member, sprawled out on our sectional with her hands in his hair, and I'd sat on the other side of the sectional, because Mom wouldn't let Abby be alone with a boy on the couch and chaperoning was my job.

So, I sat there with a pillow in my lap, over my belly, watching them out of the corner of my eye, wanting what she had so badly I ached.

"I'll be right back," I whispered and kissed his ear before sliding out from under his head. I ran to my apartment, checked my emails. Answered a few questions.

Saw my message to my sister on Facebook. She still hadn't answered, but I read it again, feeling more powerfully than yesterday that I was falling into something with Jesse. Something real.

It was embarrassing to read those words, but they were also undeniable.

I was falling in love. Or, if not love, an infatuation so complete it was like love. I didn't know the difference.

I didn't delete the message, I left it there, like a kind of statement. I could be both. I could be me, the me right now. And the me that was Abby's sister. I left the Facebook message right next to the picture of my sister and me.

And then I headed back to Jesse's apartment.

I opened my door only to find a man standing outside of Jesse's. He was tall and big, wearing a good suit. A suit far too good for this place. A suit that belonged in my old life and maybe my future life, but not this life.

His blond hair was pushed away from his face, revealing thick lobes of cauliflower ears.

"Can I help you?" I asked and he turned toward me with a smile. He was older, but very handsome. Tall and built. His nose had the distinctive curve of having been broken. One or a dozen times.

"I'm looking for Jesse Herrera."

"Can I ask what it's about?"

He smiled at me and nodded slowly. "It's good when the guys have a strong woman at their back. You're his girlfriend?"

I almost said neighbor, but swallowed it back. Because that would be ridiculous. Instead I nodded. I was. I was Jesse's girlfriend.

He pulled a card out of the pocket of his fancy suit. "I run an MMA gym in the city. And I'd like to talk to Jesse about training there."

"You're a coach?" I asked.

"I am. I'm a coach and we have some management staff. Some sponsors. We're full-service."

I glanced down at the card in my hand.

"You have a website," I said, feeling like I might hug the guy.

"We do. It's on the card with the phone number. We'd love to talk to Jesse."

"He'd love to talk to you, too," I said. But if I knew Jesse at all, which I liked to think I did, this kind of surprise interview would not go well. "Can he call you?"

"Any time!" the man said, holding his hands out wide. "I put my cell phone on there too, on the back of the card. He can call that number or the gym. He can call anytime. I haven't been this excited about a fighter since I first opened my gym."

We shook hands and I watched the big man leave, skirting the edge of the pool with its beer bottles and dead leaves.

Maybe... I thought, a bubble of glee rising up in my throat. Maybe this place wasn't for either of us anymore.

Maybe we'd get out of here together.

I opened Jesse's door and walked in just as he was walking out of his bedroom, wearing his sweatpants low on his hips and no shirt. For a moment, I stopped, struck dumb in a way. Or still, maybe. Like so much of the noise in my head just— not only quieted, but went away. Vanished.

"Everything okay?" he asked, his sleepy eyes waking up.

"You're beautiful," I said.

"You're just saying that because you want in my pants."

"I do. But...you're beautiful."

"You're beautiful too, baby," he whispered, coming to stand right up next to me, his stomach touching mine. His bare foot resting against mine. He put his hands on my hips and pulled me in even closer. I could feel him inhale. I put my hand over his heart and felt it beating into my palm. "I've never known anyone like you."

"Come on," I said, kissing his cheek. "Some nerdy girl in high school who let you cheat off her math test?"

"That was you?"

"She was me."

"Impossible. I would have seen you. I would have known you. No matter where or how—I would know you, Charlotte. You're mine."

"Does that make you mine?"

He kissed me and I tasted the answer.

Mine.

"Hey," I said, breaking the kiss. "There was a guy outside your door looking for you." I handed him the card. "He said he runs a gym in the city—"

"Jesus. Casper Gaines?" He glanced up at me, a smile spreading across his face. A smile that made my heart lift.

"He didn't say, he just said he wanted to talk to you about training. He said he hasn't been so excited about a fighter since he opened his gym."

"Ho. Ly. Shit," he breathed. "Where's my phone? I need to look up this website."

His phone was sitting next to mine on the coffee table. Both of them were dead.

"Shit," he muttered, plugging his into his charger. "It's going to take a few minutes to charge."

"Come over to my apartment," I said. "You can use Izzy."

"Izzy?" He shook his head at me, still smiling, still clearly buzzing from having this card in his life. This Casper Gaines.

"Don't make fun of me. Izzy is an important part of my life." I tossed a coy look over my shoulder as we walked out of his place.

"Whatever, weirdo."

I unlocked my door and went in first, aware all the time of that Facebook message to my sister sitting open on my desktop.

"Let me get the browser open," I said, sitting down and immediately clicking the Facebook window shut. The picture of my sister and me was still on the desktop, but I left it. It was time to tell him about my sister anyway. We could look at his gym and then I'd maybe... explain everything to him. My sister. The sociopath ex-boyfriend. All of it. No more secrets.

I grinned and pulled up the website.

"Here," I said and got out from behind Izzy so he could sit and look at the website. "You want any coffee or anything?" I asked as he sat down, his face glued to the slick dynamic website on the screen.

He was silent, eyes tracking the flashing photographs on the header.

"Right," I said with a smile and turned toward my kitchen to make some coffee.

This day...this day was going to be the best day.

———

Jesse

I had not spent any time putting names or faces or words to what I wanted. But looking at this website and knowing what I knew about Casper Gaines, I could only think... *this.*

This is what I wanted.

I wanted the gym. Gaines. I wanted his fucking sponsors. The management shit. I wanted all of it.

Charlotte put a cup of coffee on the desk at my elbow and I mumbled thanks to her. She kissed my head and said something about a shower. I clicked over onto the section about the athletes they trained.

Jesus, I thought with a smile. One of my old high school wrestling teammates was working out there. Every minute this place seemed better and better.

Charlotte's computer dinged and a Facebook messenger window popped up. I glanced down, because that was human fucking nature, wasn't it? I wouldn't have read it, but it was so short, I couldn't really help it.

Glad you're in love, sis. I'm fucking pregnant.

Shit. Ohhhh... fucking shit.

All that joy in my body died. Fell into my stomach like lead. I felt sick.

I'd put this off, I'd put it off and I pretended she wasn't who I knew she was.

Beneath the edge of the gym website I could see the bright-colored edge of a picture on her desktop, and I knew part of the picture had to be her, because of the white-blonde curls along the side.

This was it. This was how we ended.

I clicked out of the website, which left only the Facebook message and a picture on the screen.

A picture of Charlotte and someone who could only be her sister. They were twins.

They looked enough alike that they had to be twins, but Charlotte was soft where her sister was hard. Sharp, even. She didn't have Charlotte's hair. Or her smile. She had more teeth, straight hair but the exact same blonde.

Their eyes were the same—blue as blue could get.

They were wearing boas and fake princess crowns. Charlotte was holding up a cosmo, her eyes closed as her sister hugged her around the neck.

Charlotte's sister was a fucking knockout. Like model beautiful. And I saw all at once how Charlotte had acquired all her insecurities, how a life compared to this twin of hers would make her feel like she constantly came up short.

And I could also see why my brother was looking for this woman. She was exactly his type.

And she was fucking pregnant.

And Charlotte loved me?

God, I wanted to cling to that. I wanted to make the truth of those words into some kind of coat I could wear to keep out the cold of my life. I heard the shower go off in her bathroom and I wanted to go to her there and tell her I loved her too. As much as I knew how to. As much as I was able.

I wanted to tell her how grateful I was.

Too much. Too fucking much. I backed away from the desk. Got to my feet. All of this... Jesus. I couldn't keep the shitstorm raining down on me clear at the moment. Fuck. One thing at a time.

If my brother knew this girl was pregnant, there'd be no holding him back, and since Charlotte was the only person who knew where her sister was—I had to keep Charlotte as far away from my brother as possible.

Which meant she needed to move out.

For a second I allowed myself to imagine both of us

moving out. Into some better place in the city. She could make her amazing books, I could fight legitimately.

I imagined telling her who my brother was and how she would hug me and tell me his sins were not mine.

But telling her would not solve the problem of my brother looking for her sister.

We could leave the city, I thought.

But that didn't solve my brother either.

Nothing solved my brother. The problem of who I was and whose blood was in my veins—it was unsolvable.

I was who I was. A son in the family I was born into. Carrying the debts of my father and the crimes of my brother.

Because I could run—just like Charlotte's sister—but my brother always found me.

The way he broke into my apartment like he had that right—that was my life to him. A thing he could always be a part of, and I could not outrun that.

Charlotte and me were a dream. Just… just a fucking dream. And it was time to wake up.

CHAPTER FIFTEEN

Charlotte

I put on the lotion Abby gave me for Christmas. It made me smell like a stripper but I still loved it, and then I wrapped myself up in my sugar skull robe that I loved probably too much.

This was my version of combat clothes. Of a suit of armor. I needed to tell Jesse about my sister, and I wore the things I loved so I could do it and feel strong. My hair was heavy down my back, as ever my grounding force. Still wet, the curls all stretched out so my hair reached past my shoulder blades.

When I opened the bathroom door, the fog from the hot shower came out with me and when I turned into the living room I saw Jesse on his feet behind the computer.

"So?" I asked, excited for him to be excited about that gym. "What do you think?"

He jerked his chin forward at my computer. "Who is the girl? In the picture?"

Okay. We'll... just get right into it. "You...want to sit down?"

"No. I want you to tell me who this girl is?"

He was being hard and cold, and I told myself he was just angry because I'd been keeping a secret. My stomach turned sour and I forced my hands to my sides.

"My sister," I said. "My twin."

"Twins." He laughed, sharp and harsh, like he couldn't believe it.

"We don't look a whole lot alike now—"

"She's fucking hot."

It stung. I mean... it really stung. It wasn't like I hadn't been hearing that or feeling that the majority of my life, but from him, it took me out at the knees.

I wanted to shake it off as some kind of graceless moment on his part, a reaction to a startling part of my life, but it wasn't easy. For a few seconds I was speechless.

"Where is she?" he asked, tilting his head as he looked at that picture. Like she was something he was considering. I wanted to run over there and hit the power button on my monitor so he couldn't see it.

"I don' t know," I said. "She... she left town. It was really sudden. It's actually why I'm here. I had to give her some money."

"You gave her money so she could leave town and you could move into Shady Oaks?"

"It was kind of an emergency," I said.

"It was kind of fucking stupid."

He stepped out from behind my computer and I felt myself shrinking. Shrinking like I always did. Shrinking because it was easier to be invisible than it was to be visible and judged.

And it seemed like after all this time—Jesse was judging me.

Fuck, I thought. *Fuck this*. And I put my chin up.

For a second he paused at the edge of my desk, staring at me, and I waited for him to apologize, because he was a little feral, sure, but this wasn't him.

"What...? Why are you doing this?" I asked.

"You need to leave."

"It's...this is my apartment."

"No. You need to leave Shady Oaks. Like now. Do you have money?"

"What does that have to do with anything?"

"Do you have the money to get a new place?"

"Yes."

"Then do it."

"Why?"

"I'm going to go to that gym," he said, in his voice. The voice I recognized. "Check it out."

"You want me to come with?" I asked, thinking of what Casper said about strong women at the backs of these fighters.

"What the fuck are you going to do at a gym?" he scoffed, his eyes raking my body, and blood poured into my cheeks.

"Support you, asshole," I spat. "What is happening to you?"

"Everything," he said, holding his arms out, all those muscles that I'd traced with my fingers and my tongue standing out in beautiful relief. "Everything is happening to me. I'm leaving this shithole behind."

My eyebrows skyrocketed. "Are you...am I part of this shithole?" I asked.

"Not if you leave."

I gasped. I literally gasped.

"Baby," he said, stepping forward like he was going to touch me, and I shoved his hand away. "Come on. What did you think was going to happen, here? Really?"

"Not this," I said.

"Baby." He stepped closer and I stepped back, feeling like I did when he was a stranger. Like I had no idea what he was going to do. "We were never real. We were never going to be in love. You..." He swallowed. "You aren't for me. But," he grinned again, and my hand ached to smack that grin off his face. "That don't mean we can't fuck—"

"Get out." I wasn't crying, the heat of fury and embarrassment was cauterizing me on the inside.

"Charlotte..."

"Get the fuck out of my apartment."

Perhaps a tougher woman than me—for sure my sister—would have been able to say those words and look him in the eye and suffer through the crushing pain of a heart breaking —but I could not.

I stared down at that chipped tile in my kitchen and I waited for him to leave.

He stood there a second, his bare feet visible just at the edge of my vision.

"Get out!" I yelled and then he was gone.

Leaving just the scent of him in my apartment.

———

Jesse

I did everything I could in the next day to not be at my apartment. To not be near her. If I was in the apartment, listening to her hit the snooze button three times, smelling her coffee and the food she made for dinner, imagining her drawing those amazing drawings of hers, I would have crumbled. I would have knocked on her door and begged her to run away with me.

I had two giant purses, enough money to see us settled somewhere fine. Finer than I'd ever been.

But while most of that shit I'd said in her apartment had been a lie, the part about her not being for me... That was true.

So I stayed away, so I wouldn't reach for her and drag her down to where I lived.

Casper's gym was pretty fucking amazing. I met the team there. The trainers and managers. The other fighters. My old teammate told me it was a legit situation and I believed him.

Casper handed me the management contract but didn't let go of it when I tried to take it from his hand.

"I have one major stipulation," he said.

Internally, I was all edges. All growling no's. I was ready to tell him to fuck off before he even got the words out.

"What is it?" I said, with narrowed eyes.

"You have to stop the fights in the basement," he said. "They're dangerous."

It was relief that ran through me. A relief so powerful it was scary.

It's okay to want more. Charlotte said that. *To think you deserve more.*

And the old me, the me before her would have said, nope. Or maybe he would have agreed, but still found that reckless dangerous shit to do. Or maybe the old me wouldn't have even have had the balls to show up here today. I had no idea.

But the me after Charlotte, said, "No problem." Casper let go of the document. "I need to take this home with me and have some people look at it."

More of Charlotte's influence.

"Good idea," he'd said. "We're a family kind of team. I hope we'll see your girlfriend around here."

I looked at him blankly. Girlfriend?

"The beautiful blonde I met at your apartment."

Charlotte. "She's not...mine. I'm alone."

Casper's mouth pressed tight for a moment. "Well, not if you join our gym you're not."

I left the gym, my head bent against the Bay Area wind, the contract shoved in the back pocket of my jeans. And the person I wanted to talk to about all of this was Charlotte. I mean, I read the thing and it seemed like a good deal, but what the fuck did I know about good deals? Shit. I knew shit about them.

But I couldn't call Charlotte. So when I got home, I called Amber and Matt. Matt was a lawyer and he said he'd be happy to read over the contract.

Two hours later they were at my door with a bottle of vodka and some fucking horn-dog expressions on their faces.

"This isn't about that," I said as they came in.

"About what?" Amber asked, all wide-eyed as she shrugged out of her coat. She wore a thin shirt and a skirt and I knew without having to check that she'd be naked under those clothes. And wet, too.

"Fucking. We're not fucking," I said.

Amber and Matt exchanged "yeah, right" looks.

"I'm serious. I need you to look at this." I handed over the contract and Matt took it, going to sit on my couch so he could pay attention to it.

"What's with you?" Amber asked. "Matt thinks this whole change with you is about that Charlotte girl."

"She has nothing to do with anything."

Amber glanced over at Matt.

"Told you," he said without looking up. "Our boy is falling for the neighbor."

Through the paper-thin walls I could hear Charlotte moving around and then the sound of her door opening. *Don't,* I prayed. *Please, baby, don't come over here.*

It would hurt her to see Amber and Matt here. And I would be forced to hurt her more.

Go get groceries. I even closed my eyes like I was praying. *Go get that greasy diner breakfast you love. A cup of coffee. Fuck. Baby. Go on that date you were supposed to go on. Go anywhere but here.*

But then there was a knock on my door and I hung my head and swore.

Goddamn it, Charlotte.

"Jesse?" Amber asked. "Are you okay?"

"Answer the door, would you?" I whispered, trying to find in myself the strength to do what I needed to do.

Amber opened the door.

"Jes—oh, Amber," Charlotte said, and I could hear every-thing she wasn't saying. All the assumptions she was making and all the hurt they were causing her.

"Hey Charlotte. You want to come in?" Amber asked.

"No. No, it's okay. I just…" Charlotte stepped into the apartment and looked for me. "Jesse." Her face was all wrong. It was still and careful, showing me nothing, but I could still see everything underneath her skin. All her pain. All her doubt. All her anger. "I have your chair." She lifted the blue bean bag chair with both hands.

"Thanks," I said.

"Can I… can I talk to you?" she asked.

I shrugged.

"Outside?"

"Whatever you need to say you can say in front of Amber and Matt."

"Fuck," Amber said. "Jesse, don't be a dick."

Being a dick was the point. Being a dick was what I needed to do, but it was getting so hard. So hard to look at Charlotte and still put my foot down on her throat. But she needed to get the hell out of here.

"Sure," I said and stepped through the door into the hallway. I made sure to put as much distance between us as I could, but it still wasn't enough. I could smell her shampoo. I could feel the heat of her skin against the cold of mine.

"I think," she whispered, looking down at her hands for a moment. "I think maybe you saw something on my computer. A conversation I was having with my sister—"

"About how you love me and she's pregnant?"

She flinched. Like I'd punched her in the stomach, she flinched. I put my hands in fists so I wouldn't reach for her.

"Right," she said with a dry cracked voice. "I just…if that's why you're acting like this—"

"Like what?"

"Like I don't mean anything to you."

You do. You mean everything. You mean so much more than I ever thought I'd get.

"Of course you mean something to me, Charlotte. You want to come inside? We were about to go into the bedroom."

She sucked in a breath. Another one. Put a hand out against the doorjamb like she was light-headed. "Have…" she said. "Have the fucking balls to just break up with me. To just tell me that all that stuff you told me was a lie. Don't fucking stand here and gaslight me into thinking I imagined everything you said. Everything you did. The way you talked to me and held me—"

She put her face down, her hair falling over her shoulders, and I looked up at the cracked ceiling and prayed for strength.

"You know something?" she said with a hard, cold voice. "Fuck you. It doesn't matter. You're not the man I thought you were."

And then she was gone.

Her apartment door slamming shut behind her.

"You are such a dick," Amber said, coming out to stand with me in the hallway when I didn't go back in.

"You heard?" I said.

Matt came out a few seconds later. They had their vodka and coats on.

"The contract is good," he said. "It's fair. But man... Amber and I aren't tools you use to hurt another woman. You're not the guy we thought you were either."

And then they too were gone.

Funny, I thought, feeling hollow and empty. *I'm exactly the guy I thought I was.*

CHAPTER SIXTEEN

Charlotte

My skin was the only thing holding me together, when I got back to my apartment, but immediately I called my agent and told her I would go on the book tour. Whatever they wanted. Whatever events and booksignings, I'd do interviews, I'd bungee jump off buildings if that's what they wanted me to do.

I was a new person, with a new life, and this book tour would be my coming-out party.

When I hung up I felt like I was going to puke. Which, oddly, was better than I had been feeling.

My Facebook message binged.

What happened? my sister asked.

After Jesse left yesterday, I'd spent hours Facebook messaging with Abby.

It's over, I typed back.

Oh, Char. I'm really sorry.

Me too. How are you doing?

Fine. I took your advice and made a doctor's appointment. I can't keep pretending this isn't happening to me.

Good for you. Are you going to tell him?

Him being the sociopath ex-boyfriend. We didn't write about the baby, that seemed to be her rules. A thing she didn't want to talk about. Other than the first comment at the top of our conversation, there was no more discussion of her being pregnant, except in the broadest terms. Classic Abby.

No, she wrote back fast. *He can never know. Not ever.*

Is he really that bad? I asked.

He's bad enough that I'm halfway across the country with all your money just to get away from him.

Did he hurt you? I asked, settling into my worry about Abby's life because it was such a relief to take a break over worrying about mine.

No. He never hurt me. He'd never...do that. But Char, he hurts other people.

I thought of Jesse and the violence he lived with, and how shocking I understood that to be.

Sometimes things aren't always what they seem, I wrote.

I saw him kill someone.

What?!

He's a killer. Stone-cold, Char. He put a bullet in the back of someone's head.

Holy shit.

I know. It's bad. It's just... bad.

Suddenly, I realized how I could make this whole situation work. I could turn this around for both of us, these dark days could be made happy.

Abby, I typed. *Tell me where you are. I'll come to where you are. I can help. I can do this with you.*

I hit send but she didn't type anything back. Not for a long time.

Abby? I finally wrote.

Char, she wrote. *I want you to come here so bad. You have no idea. I'm crying just thinking about it. But... if you come here, we'll go right back to all the things we usually do. I'll let you take care of me instead of taking care of yourself. Instead of me taking care of myself. I have to take care of myself sometime, don't I?*

She was right. She was completely right.

And I had to take care of myself.

I was just so fucking lonely. My only friend was half a country away. The girls by the side of the pool wouldn't be out for a few more days with their juice glasses of wine. I needed a friend and I needed one now.

Hey, my sister typed because even though she was hundreds of miles away she could still read my mind. *You need to go out.*

Yeah, I typed back. *With who?*

What about that Simon guy?

I winced.

No.

Why not, she typed. *Just get out of the apartment. Go have a conversation, do anything to stop thinking about Jesse.*

That...that sounded good. A friend. No thinking about Jesse.

Okay, I typed.

Atta girl, my sister wrote.

So after putting him off for weeks—I returned Simon's phone calls.

"Hey!" he answered on the second ring. "Charlotte!"

"Hi, Simon." It was awful, I knew that, but the excitement in his voice was a certain kind of balm to the injuries Jesse had left on my soul. Perhaps this idea of Abby's wasn't half bad.

"You're out from under your deadline?" he asked. I'd cancelled on him citing deadline problems, because I'd been too awkward to say I was having crazy monkey sex with my next door neighbor.

"I am. Well, it's not done, but the pressure is off."

"Want to get that cup of coffee?"

"Can we upgrade to a glass of booze?" Or twenty.

He laughed and I closed my eyes, feeling awful, because his laughter didn't fill me with any kind of warmth. It didn't send little electric shocks through my system. It didn't make me want to smile.

But it was something, and I felt... I just felt like I had nothing right now.

"Absolutely," he said. "Tomorrow night?"

"Yes," I said.

If nothing else I would get out of the house, I wouldn't be stuck in these four walls, listening to Jesse in his four walls.

———

The next day I dressed for...war, or something. I dressed to hurt a man who didn't care. Who wouldn't even see me. This was pathetic. But it was the only thing I knew to do. It was the only thing that made me feel like I hadn't been stabbed in the stomach. Like I'd lost all my skin in a fire.

Like I wasn't disposable. Disposable to a man I cared so much for.

How did that happen? I wondered, putting lipstick on, my brightest red. How did I fall so far so fast?

My breath shuddered in my throat, but I looked myself in the eye, gave myself a shake that made all the glitter on my shirt dance. Indicating a merriment I was far from feeling. And I grabbed my purse and keys and headed out the door.

Jesse was there.

And I couldn't say I hadn't been listening for him. I couldn't completely swear that I wasn't aware he'd left his house for a run about an hour ago. Part of me cringed and part of me crowed and my subconscious, it seemed, was out for blood.

It wasn't totally an accident that I was leaving just as he was coming back.

But he hadn't been running, he was standing there with grocery bags. I saw apples and spinach. Chicken breasts. Food that would indicate he was taking care of himself.

I could have choked on my pride for him.

Our eyes met and the electric shock of it was real. It buzzed through my body, making my fingers numb and my nipples hard. Silent, I turned away to lock my door.

"Where are you going?" he asked.

I said nothing because I felt such a scream in me. Such a wild fury and pain. Best to keep it swallowed down. Best to keep it inside.

"Charlotte?"

He stepped closer, not crowding me but close enough I could feel him. My numb fingers fumbled with the key.

"I have a date."

He swore under his breath and I got my door locked and stepped away, trying to find enough air between us to breathe.

"With that nice designer?" he asked, his face flushed. His eyes hard.

"It's not your business."

"It's my business if you fuck him. If you bring him back here." He stepped closer and I stepped back so fast I hit the wall behind me. The stucco tugging at my loose hair. "You mad at me? Take it out on me."

He was close now, so close I could smell him. I could taste him when I inhaled—a salt on my tongue.

"You want to fucking tear into me?" he asked. "Let's do it. Come inside and I'll let you hurt me all you want."

"Why?" I asked, blinking at him.

He was silent, his jaw tense like he didn't know why he was offering that. Like he had to offer that. Like it was all he had. Come inside and fuck him and hurt him.

"Because you want me enough that you don't want me to fuck some other guy? It... doesn't work that way, Jesse. I don't work that way. You hurt me. You really hurt me. I'll never let you touch me again."

He went still at my words and I did too, a little bit. Stunned that I'd said those things. Stunned that I was so honest. Stunned that in letting him know how badly he'd hurt me, I actually felt better.

I felt stronger.

I didn't have to swallow down every pain every person visited upon me. I could hold my head up and let people know I was here. That my feelings mattered. That I mattered.

I'd never done that before.

"Let me go," I said, because he was crowding me against the wall. I could see him fight it, I could see him want to lean in and touch me until I agreed to go inside with him.

And for all my strong words, I wasn't sure I wouldn't do it. If he touched me, the way he knew I liked because he had that knowledge of me—I couldn't be sure I would be strong.

There was a good chance I would melt down into his hands like candle wax.

"Do you need money to move out?" he asked.

"Why the fuck do you care?"

"Because I won't be here to protect you. Because this place isn't for you. Because you're better than this fucking place and it's time for you to live like that."

He was yelling and when his eyes met mine and I saw, somehow... he was hurting too. It was there in his eyes, a regret so clear and sharp I stood up away from the wall and very nearly reached for him.

Immediately, he stepped back, turned away.

"You need to leave," he said.

Questions battered against my lips, but I'd already done so much talking. I'd already opened myself up to a thousand hurts. I couldn't do it anymore.

I could not trust that hurt I saw in his eyes, and I couldn't trust that he wouldn't deny it and hurt me again.

Silent, I walked past him and the air of the October evening was cold on my burning skin.

Once I was past the ridiculous gates out onto the street, once I could feel that he wasn't watching me anymore, I stopped and leaned against the crumbling stucco half wall. I grabbed my phone from my purse and pulled up my texts with Simon.

I'm so sorry to do this, I texted. *But I'm going to have to cancel. The truth is, I've been involved with someone else and I'm just…a little broken right now.*

He wrote back almost immediately.

It's okay, he texted. *I understand. We can get that drink as friends if you'd like.*

Thank you, but not tonight. I've got to straighten some things out in my life.

And then I pulled up Craigslist and started looking for new apartments.

And within two hours I was putting together my new life. That looked just like my old life, without the square footage or the balcony with the cheerful geraniums. In my new life I could only afford a studio in a slightly better neighborhood, and if that bothered me in some way, if that felt constraining or not exactly what I wanted, I blamed it on my shoes.

On the gray cloud over my head.

I blamed it on my heart.

———

When do you move in? my sister typed two days later. It was Friday, and I was deep into the bottle of wine I'd bought earlier. I was well aware I should have gotten two bottles. I wanted to be lights-out drunk, so I wouldn't lie awake in that bed listening to the creak of Jesse's bed through the wall.

Two weeks, I wrote back. *How is the job?*

Good, she wrote. *I'm a little surprised how much I like it here.*

Surprised? How about shocked? How about I don't even know you? You went right back to the scene of the worst family vacation in history.

We'd been fifteen and our parents had booked us on a vacation in some dude ranch mountain town, and Abby and I had thrown up a serious protest. We'd dragged our feet and rolled our eyes, but then when we'd gotten there, Abby had broken rank and ended up loving the place.

She'd volunteered to work in the barn in the mornings. My sister had actually shoveled shit.

You have no idea how good the air tastes here, she wrote.

Like horseshit?

I didn't think I'd stay here, she typed. *I thought I'd stop, look around and move on. But that Help Wanted sign was up in café and it just...seemed right.*

I have a hard time picturing you in a small town.

You and me both. But It's a relief, she typed. *He'll never find me here and the cowboys that come into the café aren't half-bad.*

That sounded like my sister.

Are you scared? I typed.

Shitless. I am scared shitless.

I settled in for a big conversation about the baby, we needed to do it. I poured what was left of my wine bottle into my glass – but it was half a sip.

Hey, I typed. *I'm going to get more wine. I'll be back in about fifteen minutes.*

You sure you should be walking around at night in your neighborhood?

There's a liquor store on the corner. I'll be fine. It's also only nine o'clock. It's not like the sun went down in South San Francisco and the zombies came out.

Just, she texted, *you have to be careful. You don't know the things Jack is capable of.*

Jack? I texted, my heart stopping mid-beat. She'd never told me the guy's name.

Yeah. Jack won't give up on finding me, Char. I saw something I shouldn't have seen and he's going to be after me. And no one will find me here, but you're still in the city and now...where you're living? I'm worried.

Don't be, I texted, though now I was worried. Jack. It had to be a coincidence? Right? I mean, it was an incredibly popular name. How many Jacks were in this city? Probably a million. Literally, a million.

Hey, she texted. *I'm going to go to bed. I'll talk with you tomorrow.*

I closed down the chat out of old habit and grabbed my keys and purse. I was drunk but not that drunk, and I got down to the liquor store in the indigo twilight and back with my bottle of pinot noir under my arm in what I was sure was record time.

I thought of the man my sister was running from and thought of all the ways I hadn't been careful. Abby had warned me, a thousand times over she'd warned me in those frantic days two months ago, to be careful. To cover my tracks. But walking back to the apartment complex all I could see was the tracks I'd left behind as I made my way into hiding. The tracks my sister had left. Credit card receipts for the hotel and the crappy pickup truck she bought. And we probably should have dyed our hair or something. Changed our appearances. My hair alone was kind of a calling card.

And then...there was the matter of Jesse's brother. A dangerous man named Jack.

Maybe it was because I was drunk, or maybe it was because I'd grown some balls living in Shady Oaks, I couldn't be sure, but instead of going to my apartment I went to Jesse's.

I knocked on the door, ready to get some answers about his brother.

About my sister.

Us, maybe.

I knocked and I knocked but he didn't answer. In the end I went back to my apartment and drank most of that second bottle of wine.

But no matter how much I drank, my skin felt tight.

And it was impossible to breathe.

———

The next day I was hungover, walking home with some Chinese takeout, the drizzling rain making everything seem so much worse that it really was. My head was down and when I got to my door I pulled my keys out of my pocket, shifted my fried rice to my other hand and stepped forward to open my door.

But it was already open.

My breath caught. My heart pounded so hard I could feel it in my eyes.

I swallowed the sudden copper taste of fear in the back of my throat and leaned sideways, looking through the open crack of my door. I couldn't see anyone and for a second I took a breath. But then from inside I heard something crash to the floor and break and I jumped sideways, a hand over my mouth. Terror making me dizzy. I took three stumbling steps over to Jesse's door and I sent up a wild prayer.

Please, please be home.

Please, please hear this almost-silent knock on your door.

I knocked again, heard another crash from my apartment and I got ready to run. Run anywhere.

But Jesse's door opened and at the sight of his familiar face and his strong body I nearly melted in relief.

"Char—"

I shook my head and shoved him inside. Closing the door behind us. I leaned back against it, shaking so hard the bag of Chinese food fell from my hands.

"Jesus, baby," he breathed, grabbing my shoulders in his hands. "What happened? Are you all right?"

Oh God, that his touch had the power to make me feel better. His touch had the power to force my body back into working. All systems repaired.

"There is someone in my apartment," I breathed.

"What?"

"Someone... is in my apartme—" I didn't even finish it a second time before Jesse was carefully moving me aside. He ran out the door and I heard him in my apartment, but it was quiet. No shouting. No fighting. No sound of anyone else in there.

I bent forward at the waist, my hands at my knees, trying to suck in deep breaths. The smell of my Chinese food on the floor beneath me was now making me sick.

"Charlotte." Jesse's voice when he came back inside was quiet. Calm. "Whoever was in there is gone. They broke... they broke your computer."

I crumbled onto the floor. Izzy... oh God, Izzy.

Jesse picked me up in his arms and carried me to the couch. "It's okay," he whispered into my hair. "I think it's just the monitor."

I stood up. "The picture."

"What picture?"

"My sister. The picture of us on the monitor. And our Facebook messages. I have to go—"

I darted past him, but he grabbed me. I smacked at his hands with all the hurt and rage I felt until he wrapped his arms around me, locking my hands against my sides. "Listen," he said into my ear.

"No. I'm not listening to anything you say. Ever."

"It's my brother she's running from."

The confirmation of all my worst fears felt like a penny dropping into a machine.

"I know," I spat. Holding myself rigid in his arms, refusing to feel any of his body against mine.

"How do you know?" he asked. I didn't, really, not until this minute.

"My sister told me the man she's running from was a man named Jack. A sociopath killer."

"And you just assumed it was my brother?"

"Perhaps sociopathy runs in your family."

That was mean and I regretted it the second I said it.

"Let me go," I whispered.

"You can't run. Not until we have a plan."

"We don't have anything," I spat.

"It's your sister and my brother. Don't you think we should figure something out?"

"Fine. I won't...run."

He let me go in pieces. First his hands let go of my hands and his arms let go of mine, and then his body, thick and warm and strong, stepped away from mine and I was cold. I was so damn cold without him.

I turned, shaking my loose hair out of my eyes, and he looked somehow smaller all of a sudden. As if he'd been compressed and squeezed.

"Did you know? About him and my sister? All this time?"

"I knew my brother was looking for the sister of a woman

he'd been involved with. I didn't know for sure it was you until I saw that picture and the messages between you on your computer."

"But you suspected..."

He nodded, looking guilty as fuck.

I leaned back against the door, surprised he could hurt me. Surprised I could feel anything but fear. "Is that why you started seeing me?"

"Yes."

I laughed or I tried to, but it came out as a sob. I had to get the hell out of here. Away from him.

"But that's not why I stayed," he said. "You have to believe that."

"I don't care," I said, reaching for the door. But he was there, his hand on mine, his body a strong wall behind me. Every part of my body wanted to lean against him. Warm myself against him, for just a second...to just prepare myself for the long cold days ahead.

"I was falling in love with you," he said.

"Stop."

"I was."

"Stop!" I shrieked and I pushed at him. I shoved at him. Again and again until we were back in his living room. "You don't get to say that now. Not now."

"I saw that picture of you and your sister and I knew who she was. Who you were."

"So you hurt me on purpose?" I was crying, despite trying not to.

"I hurt you on purpose. Because he's my brother. And as long as you're with me, you won't be safe. No one is safe."

That made me stop. Still.

"Are you safe?" I asked.

He licked his lips, a nervous tick that somehow made me scared and hot at the same time. "He's not the brother I knew," he said. "And I don't...don't know what he'll do anymore. That's why you need to leave."

"What about you?"

"It doesn't matter where I go," he said. "He's my brother. We always find our way back to each other."

This was it. This was how we ended.

"My sister fell in love with some guy she met at a restaurant downtown," I said. "She didn't tell me anything about him, I'm not sure how much she knew about him. Just that she was in love and he was the most amazing man she'd ever met and she'd never felt that way before. But Abby was prone to feeling that way, you know. She loves big and fast—like a building going up in flames. And then, about two months ago she shows up on my doorstep, freaking out because she's got to leave town. Like that night she has to leave town. She had a bag with her and a thousand dollars in cash and she was saying goodbye. Just like that."

"What did you do?" he asked.

"Got her to stay an extra week, sold my condo, gave her most of everything I had and moved here."

"Jesus," he breathed. "No questions asked?"

"She's my sister. She didn't ask for it, but she needed it and she was running. Scared for her life, from your brother. She told me I had to be careful. Lie low."

"Shady Oaks is pretty low," he said, with a wry smile that made him look so young. "Just shit luck you moved in next to me."

"I don't... it wasn't shit luck. It—" I closed my eyes and took a deep breath. "You're one of the most amazing things that's ever happened to me."

His eyes when he looked at me were so bright I almost thought he was about to cry. "No one has ever said that to me."

I shrugged, because what else could I say. "You going to tell me what happened with your brother?"

"We don't have time," he said. "We've got to get you out of here. Go back to your place and pack up only what you need. I'll get your computer in my car and we'll get you out of here."

He opened the door, swinging it open only to reveal the rainy day and a man standing in the hallway who looked so much like Jesse.

Too much.

"Going somewhere, brother?"

Jack.

CHAPTER SEVENTEEN

Jesse

Two things were true in that moment:

One: I had no idea what my brother would do. He could kill me. He could absolutely kill Charlotte. The man in front of me was a stone-cold stranger wearing my brother's face.

Two: I would die to protect Charlotte.

That I'd tried to push her away seemed impossible to me now. She was somehow a part of me. Right under my skin.

"What do you want?" I asked Jack.

I opened the door a little wider, blocking Jack's view of Charlotte. I wanted her to have the sense to go hide in the bedroom. The bathroom. Anywhere. But she only stood there partially behind the door. Her eyes wide in her pale face.

"You know what I want. I want your neighbor. The blonde with the tits." He made to step in but I wouldn't let him.

He lifted his eyebrows, his lips pursed. "It's like that, is it?"

"It's like that."

Jack pulled a gun from the pocket of his long overcoat and the fucking grief of it tore me in two. Right in two.

"It's still like that," I said, letting him know he'd have to kill me before I let him hurt Charlotte.

He turned the gun so it was facing the door, the barrel pointed right at Charlotte's head, like he'd known where she would be hiding.

"It doesn't have to happen like this," he said. "Just let me in."

"You hurt her and I will kill you."

He smiled and then nodded. "I am duly warned."

I stepped backwards and Jack stepped in, shutting the door behind him. Immediately he looked at Charlotte and the smile... I shook my head, wondering if adrenaline wasn't making me see shit. Because that smile was the brother I remembered. The boy with the long hair he refused to cut. The smart kid helping me learn fractions. The shitty wrestler who kept going out on that mat because he liked being on a team with me.

Jesus. What was going on?

"Charlotte," he said, with a hint of the old charm. "You are just as your sister described you."

Charlotte, my brave bold girl, looked at the gun in his hand and sneered. "And you're just as she described you. A dangerous sociopath."

Smoothly, I got between them. I wanted to tell Charlotte not to poke the beast, but Jack seemed unprovoked. In fact he just seemed...weary. He put the gun in his pocket but the threat was already in the air.

Jack looked at me with a sad little grin on his face. "It looks like we've fallen in love with sisters. It's so ironic, isn't it? I mean the odds have to be...what, one in seven million?"

"My sister doesn't love you," Charlotte said. "She ran away from you because she's scared of you."

"I know," Jack said. "I know. I wanted... I wanted to protect her from that part of my life."

"You did a shit job of that."

"Maybe," I muttered over my shoulder, "don't provoke the guy with the gun?"

Jack pulled the gun out of his pocket and took the clip out of it and showed it to us.

"Empty," I said, surprised.

"Yeah," he breathed and threw the gun and the empty clip on the table. "I've been carrying that fucking thing around for two years, most of the time without any bullets. Praying I didn't have to use it."

"That," Charlotte breathed, "sounds awful."

"Not as awful as actually using it," he said quietly, staring down at his hands before looking up at me. "I'm out," he said. "Out of the life. I'm leaving tonight. Debts are paid. I'm...done."

"You're leaving South San Francisco?" I asked, somehow stunned to hear it.

"I'm going to find Abby," Jack said.

The air around my brother turned cold. Like ice. Did he know about the baby? I sure as hell wasn't going to say anything, and no way would Charlotte say anything either. The baby was Abby's secret.

"You won't," Charlotte said.

Jack turned toward her like a shark smelling blood on the water. I got further between them. "Touch her and I'll kill you."

"You think I'm going to beat her sister's whereabouts out of her?" Jack asked.

"I think you're capable of it."

Jack nodded, his jaw tight, like it was his due. Like he shouldn't expect any better.

"I have a pretty good idea where she is," he said. "She told me about that vacation your family took when you were fifteen. The ranch and the small town."

"Well, if you do find her, she won't have anything to do with you. At all."

Jack's chest lifted with a soundless laugh. "That is much more likely. Why does she need the doctor?" he asked. "Is she all right?"

"I'm not telling you shit," Charlotte said, and I realized Jack didn't know Abby was pregnant.

"I will find out for myself soon enough," Jack said, sounding ominous as hell.

"What are you doing here?" I asked. "If you're leaving, if you're out of the life, why are you here?"

He looked at me like I'd wounded him. "I was feeling... nostalgic, I guess. I missed my little brother. Is it so unreasonable to want to say goodbye?"

"We haven't been brothers in a long time," I said. "We're done. I don't know you."

"We've been done since Dad died," Jack said, the words bitten off like bullets from his mouth. "The second you dropped out and gave up."

"Fuck off, Jack," I said. "I came home to help you pay off the debt!"

"I didn't need you to do that!" he cried. "I needed you to stay in Iowa. I needed you to stay safe. I needed you—"

"I needed you!" I yelled, the words ripped from my gut. All I'd ever needed in my life was my brother, and he... well, fuck. I guess I didn't need him anymore, after all.

Jack nodded, his throat working hard as he swallowed. "I know. I know and all I can say is I'm sorry. I thought I was doing the right thing." He took a deep breath and looked me in the eye. "Tell her, tell her everything. If you want a shot with her, you've got to tell her. And if she stays after that... don't let her go." Jack then turned to Charlotte. "I'm sorry this is how we've met. I hope... well, let's just say I hope a lot of things."

Jack nodded at me and for a moment, stark and real, I wanted to tell him not to leave. But that was the kid in me, the little brother he'd shut out. We'd never get back what we had. I just had to hope somehow, in some way, he'd get back to being the man he used to be.

"Bye Jack," I murmured and he was gone.

I shut the door behind him.

"Oh God," Charlotte said, sucking in air. She fell back against the wall and pulled out her cell phone. "I have to warn her. I have to tell her to run." She sobbed once, hard. Tapping away on her phone.

"I don't think it will matter," I said, pulling over a chair from my shitty kitchen table. "Jack will find her."

"She's pregnant," Charlotte said, looking at me through her cloud of hair.

"He doesn't seem to know."

"He will soon enough," she said, sounding panicked. "I mean, she's having the fucking hitman's baby."

"He's not a hitman anymore," I said.

"Like that matters."

Solid point.

She put the phone down on the table and blew out a long breath.

"That's... that's it, right? I've done everything I can?"

"You've done everything you can. He won't hurt her," I told her, knowing that in my gut. Jack was a lot of things, but he didn't hurt women.

"I...I don't think he'll touch her. But I still think he can hurt her." She looked away, tucking hair behind her ears, and here we were, right back in this thing between us.

"You think he'll hurt her, like I hurt you?" I asked and she nodded. "I was trying to protect you from Jack. And my whole family thing."

"You could have just told me. Whatever it is..."

This is what my brother meant, the thing I had to tell her if we were going to stand a chance. And I was surprised by how much I wanted that chance.

Needed it.

Ached for it.

I pivoted my chair and reached for her, pulling her so close her knees were in between mine. I pulled up another chair and made her sit in it. Which she did, and then she didn't move, and I realized, my heart in my throat, that she wanted this, too. She was nervous and scared and I was going to have to work for it, but she wanted this, too.

Do. Not. Blow. This.

"My mom died when we were teenagers." Telling this story was like an archaeological dig, or something, like I was pulling up the Titanic for her.

"I'm sorry."

"It was rough. She left a real hole in our family and my dad... I don't think he ever recovered. After she died, Jack and I pretty much raised ourselves. It's not like we were kids. We were both in high school, he was on his way to college."

"Your brother was in college?"

"Business school. UCLA."

Her jaw dropped and I smiled, touching her chin like I was pushing her jaw closed. "Sorry," she said. "I just... the man who had a gun on me was accepted into UCLA business school?"

"I know. You have to understand, he was a different person then. Anyway, he went, I finished high school and went to Iowa on scholarship, and I just…I fell apart. Without my brother or my mom or anyone keeping me on the straight and narrow I just couldn't do it. School was so hard. Making friends. All of it. Everything except wrestling was too hard to even deal with. My dad was doing the same thing back here, only he was gambling. Hard. Really… serious money to some serious fucking people. And by the time Jack and I found out about it, it was too late."

"Too late how?"

"Dad was dead. Shot in the back of the head and left by the side of the highway."

"Oh my god."

"Well, it gets… it gets kind of worse. He left behind a debt. Like… five hundred thousand dollars. And if we didn't pay that money, we were going to be killed."

This time when her jaw fell open, she shut it herself. I kept talking. "I came back here and started fighting, giving every purse I won to the shitbags that held Dad's debt, but it wasn't enough. It wasn't close enough. So Jack…"

"Went to work with them."

I nodded. "At first it was just collection shit. Muscle kind of nonsense. He went deeper and deeper into it and I couldn't get him out. I couldn't reach him and he didn't want me to, so I just stopped trying. And then, sometime in the last few months, he must have killed someone."

"That's what my sister saw."

"Anyway, I guess the debt is paid."

"That's why you were taking those fights with those guys. The money."

I shook my head. "It was stupid."

Suddenly, like the earth opened up and sunlight literally filled my apartment, Charlotte was off her chair and in my lap. I grabbed her, I grabbed her so hard and so fast there was no way she was getting away from me. Not ever again.

"Nothing you've done has been stupid. You were just trying to help your brother."

I saw us all of a sudden. How alike we were because we'd been forged by our siblings, by the fire of their mistakes. The fire of our own mistakes.

We were full of cracks and fault lines, but we matched. Where she was weak, I was strong. And where I was weak... God, she was so strong.

She stroked my face, her fingers running over my hair in a way I felt down my back and across my dick. I wanted to fuck her so bad. I wanted to mark her and own her and I wanted her to mark me.

Own me.

"What happens now?" I asked.

"Well, I think I'm going to take you over to my bedroom and fuck you."

I groaned with relief, I sagged with it. I fell against her body so thankful she would have me back. So paralyzed by my good fortune.

"I've agreed to that book tour," she said. "It will be next summer."

"I've signed up at the gym," I told her. "I start on Monday. All of it. I'm taking care of myself and I'm going to stop the fights in the basement and move out of this place. And, Charlotte, listen to me, I never would have done that without you."

"Yes, you would have. You would have found your way to that gym. You wanted that."

"But the rest of it? I never would have had that faith in myself. I never would have believed I deserved it without you."

"That's how I feel about the book tour. I did it because I was mad at you, but really you just gave me the strength to see how I deserved it."

"You deserve everything. Everything you want."

"I want you."

Humbled, I rubbed my face against hers. "Say it again."

"I want you. I will always want you. Even when I hated you I wanted you."

"That's sex."

She shook her head, her curls falling down around us, a cocoon of us. "That's you. The power of you."

"The power of us," I said.

"You've wanted me too? This last week?"

"That fucking date you went on?"

"Cancelled."

I blew out a breath I felt like I'd been holding since I saw her so beautiful for another man. "Thank fuck."

She laughed, a bright sound, filling my apartment with something good.

"Is this love?" I asked. Because I didn't know. The only person I'd ever loved just walked out that door a practical stranger.

"I don't know," she said truthfully. "I've never felt like this before."

"Me neither."

"Maybe it's falling in love," she said.

"I want to be falling in love with you for the rest of my life." I'd never said anything I'd meant more.

Her eyes filled with tears and she nodded.

"You," she said, looking deep and hard into my eyes where I felt my own tears building. "Are the best fucking neighbor I've ever had."

———

Ready to find out why Abby is running from Jack and if he

finds her and the baby? (Plus more of Jesse and Charlotte)
Pick up BABY, COME BACK

Want to know more about the enigmatic Bates and how he became the dark king of San Fransisco? Pick up LOST WITHOUT YOU

Keep reading for a sneak peek at BABY, COME BACK

Keep reading for a sneak peek of Baby, Come Back

––––––––

BABY, COME BACK
ABBY
BEFORE

I'm not smart about a lot of things, but I know chemistry. Not the stuff in schools, with the beakers and everything; that's a total gong show for me. I didn't even get to Chemistry in high school because I was stuck in freshman Physical Science for four years. Thank God we got a new teacher my senior year, otherwise I never would have passed. Out went Mrs. Baker and in came handsome young Mr. Suarez.

Mr. Suarez did not stand a chance against me.

That he didn't give me an A was probably the thing he clung to at night when the guilt got to be too much for him.

Mr. Suarez was a lesson in *my* kind of chemistry.

The kind that bubbles out of thin air between two particular people. The irresistible attraction that sweeps strangers up in a current, bringing them together despite anything in the way. The kind of chemistry that changes everything.

That's something I understand, down to the ground.

It's my job, really. Or understanding it is what makes me good at my job.

Knowing when someone is looking my way a little bit longer than necessary, and how to manipulate it and feed it and then turn that into money—it's my one skill.

And I'm fucking amazing at it.

Knowing the men to avoid and the women to befriend—it's like a superpower. Chemistry is the secret that turns the world around.

Fuck love.

It's chemistry that gets shit done.

Like an idiot, I thought I knew attraction inside out, from every angle—when you only have one skill, you tend to lean on it pretty hard.

But then I met Jack.

And it wasn't love at first sight—that's for children and idiots. For people who don't fuck their high school science teacher just so they can pass a class.

It wasn't even fear at first sight. That came much later.

But it was chemistry, so much chemistry my whole world blew up.

And me with it.

BABY, COME BACK

A NOTE FROM M. O'KEEFE

Thank you so much for reading BAD NEIGHBOR. I hope you enjoyed it! Please consider leaving a review – reviews, good or bad, are super important to authors and readers!

The sequel Baby, Come Back is available now.

Want to know how Bates became the Dark King of San Fransisco? Pick up THE DEBT SERIES.

LOST WITHOUT YOU

WHERE I BELONG

RUIN YOU

Sign up for my newsletter to get all the latest news and sale announcements:

http://www.molly-okeefe.com/subscribe/

Made in United States
North Haven, CT
01 February 2022

15494843R00124